anthologies previously published by
Northants Writers' Ink

Tales of the Scorpion
While Glancing through a Window
Talking without being Interrupted
And Ghosts Are Real Too
Soft Shadows, Faint Footprints

In This County...

an anthology of stories
set in Northamptonshire

Northants Writers' Ink

edited and introduced by
Michael J Richards
Chair, Northants Writers' Ink

All material copyright © each named writer 2025
Introduction copyright © Michael J Richards 2025

All rights reserved.

This is a work of fiction. Names, characters, places and incidents are either the product of the author's imagination or are used fictitiously. Any resemblance to living persons, events or locales is entirely coincidental.

ISBN: 9798263502065

This book is available in print
and e-book versions from Amazon.

It is also available in print version
directly from Northants Writers' Ink
via its website, www.northantswritersink.co.uk
or email northantswritersink@outlook.co.uk

CONTENTS

Introduction   Michael J Richards   1

In the Past

Remember, Remember   Christopher J Wright   11

The Devil's Work   Kristian Longden   19

By Now, Darkness Has Fallen   Michael J Richards   41

An Unknown Man   Tracy Smith   65

The Silver Hornet   Gemma Croucher   89

In The Present

Moving On   Ashley Holthofer   103

Family   Jo Purdon   121

In the Future

The Formula for Culinary Success   Deborah Bromley   147

A Load of Old Cobblers   Jethro Punter   159

Your Life in Their Hands   Deborah Bromley   179

A Roar of the Engine, a Puff of Smoke   C J Wright   193

In the Beyond

Introducing Master Ajax Ambrose	Allan Shipham	213
Roses around the Door	Pat Aitcheson	227
Alone	Jason McClean	237

About the Authors   261

Introduction

In This County... is the sixth anthology published by Northants Writers' Ink, a writers' group from Wellingborough, Northamptonshire, England. It is its third to feature stories set in the county.

Divided into four sections, it comprises fourteen stories.

"In the Past", includes stories set in the early seventeenth century – Ashby St Ledgers during the Gunpowder Plot and Northampton at the time of the Witch Burnings. Then we go to mid-eighteenth century Guilsborough and 1930s Hardingstone for two real murders. Finally, in this section, a comedy of crime set in 1980s Northampton.

"In the Present" opens with a young man's search for the meaning of life in Northampton. An examination of the concept of family travelling the breadth of the county follows.

Four more stories feature in "In the Future". First, we have a delicious satire on celebrity chefs based in Silverstone. Then, in a far distant time, when Earth is flattened, a new generation chases long-forgotten

Northamptonshire myths and legends in its tunnels. After that, a savage dystopian vision of how AI will administer the county's health. Finally, in this section, a nostalgic experience of what driving cars is like compared to how it will be in twenty-five years' time.

The fourth section, "In the Beyond", brings us a magical tale starting in 1930s Wellingborough, taking us to the present day and leaving us wondering where we will go next. Then we visit some of the county's haunted places in search of spiritual comfort and rest. Our anthology concludes in Kettering where a tragic, abandoned ghost guides two young people in their journey for love and happiness.

Every story in this anthology is filled with high energy and vigorous writing. What is most surprising is the variety – true crime, historical recreations, high farce, low comedy, love, grief, bewilderment – it's all here. And more, much more.

Readers will have to search far and for a long time to find such high-quality writing similar to that found in *In This County*…

* * * * *

Our writers are, in order of appearance –

Christopher J Wright chooses to write in the speculative genre, whether it be the re-created reality of historical events or what the future might bring us.

In "Remember, Remember", he takes us to the

early seventeenth century to the final days of Robert Catesby, the mind behind the Gunpowder Plot, and to where it all began, Ashby St Ledgers, near Daventry.

His second piece, "A Roar of the Engine, a Puff of Smoke", looks to the future. In a glorious whiff of futuristic nostalgia, he imagines how we'll be driving cars in twenty-five years from now.

Christopher is the group's Treasurer.

Kristian Longden's contribution to this anthology, "The Devil's Work", gives us a scabrous picture of life in early seventeenth-century Northampton.

The fascinating aspect of this is that everything is described from the point of view of a grief-stricken and confused widower who finds himself caught up in witch trials, drunkenness, violence on his own doorstep – and deep disturbance in his own mind.

The maturity, vision and expressiveness of this writing are remarkable.

Michael J Richards writes about crime, horror and associated moral questions.

His story, "By now, darkness has fallen", portrays an horrific crime committed in Guilsborough in the mid-eighteenth century.

Tracy Smith has a talent for discovering events and locations and re-imagining them from unusual points of view.

Here, she has taken the infamous Blazing Car Murder of 1931 – the killing of an unknown man in Hardingstone by Alfred Rouse, who then tried to pretend the dead body was him.

"An Unknown Man" is written as if from the mind of Rouse himself, a challenge Tracy takes up with imaginative skill and intelligent perceptiveness. She succeeds admirably.

Gemma Croucher is new to publishing.

"The Silver Hornet" is her first published story. It is very much in the mould of her writing style – accurately observed and looked at from a sidelong viewpoint. Gemma is fully aware of the human comedy that life gives us if we care to look close enough.

Northants Writers' Ink is pleased to welcome her to the anthology.

Ashley Holthofer's story, "Moving On", is his first published story.

It explores the theme of whether human existence has meaning outside of one's own mind and subjectiveness. Ashley writes from a panoramic and epic viewpoint, his narrative style ensuring that every word works hard to earn its place in every sentence.

Northants Writers' Ink is pleased to welcome him to the anthology.

Jo Purdon likes to write about those on the fringes of

society – the minorities, the outsiders.

"Family" is a warm, compassionate story of the abandoned and abused who come together to discover love within themselves. Whatever the odds, they don't give up. They find kindness, generosity and, above all, a profound sense of family.

Jo was the first-prize winner of the Northants Writers' Ink 10th Anniversary Short Story Competition for her thrilling story, "The Hairiest High".

Deborah Bromley likes alerting us to the horrors of a future over which human beings no longer have control. Her visions of dystopian futures take no prisoners. Equally, her sharp satiric wit leave us wondering whether things will be as funny as she makes them out to be or whether the satire hides uncomfortable truths. It's both, of course.

"The Formula for Culinary Success" shows us what happens when robots take over the kitchen at an event at Silverstone. It's written as satire but the awful thing is it's probably true about the present.

"Your Life in Their Hands" is a harsh tale of hospital treatment going seriously wrong.

Deborah is the group's Secretary and Webmaster.

Jethro Punter's style is sardonic, modest understatement which hides a sharp and well-informed mind. He prefers to write about myth (which he sometimes creates himself) with one foot firmly entrenched in the magic realism genre. He also writes children's fiction.

In "A Load of Old Cobblers", he takes an idea – the tunnels of Northampton – he wrote about in the group's previous anthology, *Soft Shadows, Faint Footprints,* and develops it into a labyrinth of myth and comedy.

Allan Shipham's eternal love of the comic, the mythic and the ghostly come together in "Introducing Master Ajax Ambrose".

On the face of it, this story shouldn't succeed. An old man tells his young grandchildren of events in 1930s Wellingborough, blending ghostly happenings, futuristic magic and time travel. But it succeeds triumphantly.

Allan is one of the founder members of Northants Writers' Ink and has been published in all six of the group's anthologies.

Pat Aitcheson specialises in writing about the ungraspable yet easily understood ideas of those experiences we all have at one time or another but which, at the same time, are beyond our reach.

Such ideas as unprovable notions that we are protected by our other selves; the magic of nature; and the effect of being cared for by unseen beings, unidentifiable spirits.

In "Roses around the Door", Pat takes us through to the other side to meet those who have loved us, who wait for us to make contact and help us understand why we are here.

Jason McClean's writing is characterised by its offbeat approach. He likes to write about mythical beings and creatures. His style is no-nonsense and punchy. His compassion always shows through.

"Alone" could not have been written by anyone else. The skill lies in being able to combine communication with a disturbed spirit from the nether world via mobile phone, a tale of century-old violence and abuse and a present-day love story set in Kettering. And it works so well, so well.

More details about each author can be found in "About the authors" at the end of this book.

* * * * *

Northants Writers' Ink is a writers' group based in Wellingborough, Northamptonshire.

The first three anthologies the group published – *Tales of the Scorpion*, *While Glancing through a Window*, *Talking without Being Interrupted* – are no longer available through the usual retail channels. Previously loved copies can be found on eBay.

The fourth anthology, *And Ghosts Are Real Too*, comprises ghosts stories set in Northamptonshire. The fifth, *Soft Shadows, Faint Footprints*, are also stories set in Northamptonshire but, this time, no ghosts.

More details of these two anthologies can be found at the end of this book.

In This County… is the group's sixth anthology and its best to date.

More information about the writers' group can be found on its website www.northantswritersink.co.uk or by emailing northantswritersink@outlook.com.

* * * * *

My thanks and gratitude go to Debbie and Chris, my production team, for their full and committed support. Without them, this volume would not have been published.

Michael J Richards
Chair, Northants Writers' Ink
Editor, *In This County…*

September 2025

In the Past

Remember, Remember

Christopher J Wright

King James has decreed that all must gather to remember the deliverance of the nation from a treasonous plot. The decree is for church services but it grows more elaborate with each passing year.

I, Anne Catesby, as a Catholic recusant and a devoted mother, ignore it all, of course. But the fifth of November is a day I would never forget, even if I could. It was the last day that I saw my son, Robert, upon this Earth.

It had been a chill autumn day in the year 1605 of Our Lord, spent with the Steward in preparing the Ashby St Ledgers estate for winter. I was taking time for prayer and reflection in the solar before the evening meal, warming myself before a crackling fire, when the commotion began.

My reverie was broken by the sound of heavy footsteps crunching on the gravelled path outside the house.

"Riders!"

I heard the main door to the house open.

"Riders!"

There were footsteps on the stairs and one of the gatekeepers, Stephen, burst into the room, usual formalities dispensed with. "Riders, my lady, approaching the gatehouse."

I closed my Bible and put it on the table by my chair. "How many?"

"A half dozen, perhaps more."

"Thank you, Stephen. Go, attend to the defences."

He left the room, leaving the door ajar. The clamour of preparations rose from the lower floor. Footsteps rushing hither and thither, window shutters being swung into place, the sound of metal against metal as swords were gathered from their racks.

The riders could be priest hunters come to make another raid on Catholic recusants. But we had no clergy staying with us currently. Perhaps they were outlaws, hoping to prey on a weakly defended manor house? If so, they would not find us easy pickings.

I went to the window to peer out.

It was dark outside, it being the sixth hour after noon. But I could see lanterns slowly approaching along the lane towards the gatehouse. Surely no robbers would come in so open, yet measured, a manner as this. At length, as the riders drew close, they disappeared from my sight. There was no musket fire or any sounds of a struggle that I could hear. But my heart beat heavily as I waited on the outcome.

Soon a figure hurried towards the house. It was Stephen. I hastened out of the room and down the stairs. As I neared the last of the steps, the front door opened.

"My lady," Stephen blurted out, "it's Master Robert. He asks to speak with you at the gatehouse."

"The gatehouse? Why? No matter. Tell him I shall join him."

"Yes, my lady." Stephen pulled the door to as he left.

Gathering my winter cloak from its stand, I wrapped it around me to ward off the November air.

The gatehouse was only a hundred or so paces from the main house and I strode towards it, shivering, despite my cloak. Why would Robert not come to the house?

As I drew close, I saw movement through the windows of the gatehouse's upper room. Several men were there, bearing witness to Stephen's assessment of their numbers.

I entered the gatehouse, climbed the stairs and pushed the door open. I was taken aback by the chaotic scene before me.

Robert, still wearing a mud-spattered riding cloak, was slouched at one of the chairs by the large table that dominated the room.

I recognised Thomas Wintour, John Wright and his brother Christopher among the other men present.

"My son," I called, "what brings you home in such a manner and in such company?"

Robert rose and approached me. "Madam, forgive

my late intrusion."

He seemed worn from the ride but, more than that, he looked drawn in a way I had not seen since his father's death.

I stepped forward and touched his arm. "Robert? What has happened?"

Grasping my arm in return, he drew me away from the others. "Forgive me, Mother. I fear we are undone. One of our number has been arrested in London."

"Arrested? On what grounds?"

He did not avert his gaze as he replied, "Treason."

My thoughts went to the comings and goings of recent months, the meetings Robert had been having in the gatehouse and the time he had spent away from Ashby. I had known that something had been developing, of course, just as Robert knew that I often sheltered priests.

"Oh, Robert. What have you done?"

"We were planning to throw off the oppression of King James."

I could not contain a gasp at his words. It was treason indeed.

Robert's eyes widened at my reaction but continued. "He promised so much for the Catholic cause but he has proven worse than Elizabeth."

My head reeled as I took in what he had said. "There will be consequences. You will bring a torrent of reprisals upon our family and our faith."

"All is not lost, Mother," he said. "There will be a

groundswell of support from our Catholic neighbours. I have to send letters to the families in the area. We need supplies and fresh horses. We must depart quickly. There is a gathering planned."

"Tell me no more, Robert. I cannot know any details."

I called to Stephen. "Go to the kitchens. Have them bring pottage and ale for our guests. Have bread and cold meats prepared for travel. Send for two of the stable hands to attend to us. Move."

He hurried from the room and down the stairs.

I turned back to Robert. "Oh, my son, could you not have waited for the Lord to answer our prayers? It is presumptuous to try to force His hand like this."

"I wish only to be a tool in His right hand. The true church and its people are mistreated so widely and so basely. We do God's will."

I reached up to touch his cheek, smoothing a stray lock. "But at what cost, my son?"

"Have faith, Mother. The Lord will not desert us."

Two stable hands came in, bowing. Robert produced a handful of letters from a leather saddlebag, each already addressed and sealed.

"I need these delivered at once," he told them, "with all the haste you dare at night. They should respond with a yea or a nay. Return with their answers."

Robert divided the letters between the two men, directing which estates they should visit as they could not read the names upon them. The stable hands departed in haste.

Soon afterwards, servants arrived carrying a large pot of stew, some bread and mulled wine. Robert and his companions attacked the fare with vigour, the prospect of a hot meal and a warm fire lifting them from weary silence. Conversation broke out among them.

One of the servants guided me to a place set for me at the table and placed a bowl and some mulled wine before me. This was not what had been planned for our meal but it would do. Despite my new worries, having Robert home unexpectedly was a blessing that I welcomed.

"Are you pursued, Robert?" I said at last. "Will High Sheriff Freeman from Northampton or the King's Men from London be paying us a visit soon?"

"I don't believe so, Mother. The man who has been apprehended, Fawkes, is a seasoned campaigner and steadfast in his faith. He will not willingly give us away."

"He is still but a man and all men give out eventually."

"Perhaps," Robert said. "The government were suspicious but they had no inkling that this company was involved. Even if Fawkes breaks, events will have run their course by then."

"Events? You have more planned?"

Robert nodded, a gleam in his eye. "London was to be our most dramatic act and its loss is no small thing. But the seeds for a wider uprising are already sown. Within a week, England will be a very different country."

"I pray that you are right," I said. "But I fear the repercussions that the Protestants will heap upon us should things not turn out as you plan. I have spent much of my life and my power doing what I can to protect this family. I would not have it undone."

"Do not fear, Mother. I know the careful path you tread. Should there be the need, we will say that we passed through here quickly, not entering the house, which is true. There will be no suspicions cast upon you.

"But that will not come to pass, in any case," he assured me. "Our cause is just and will prevail."

The food and the wine were continuing to lift the spirits of the assembled men. The conversation grew in frequency and volume and I could not help but watch my son among his friends with pride. He was tall, full of vigour and assurance. He was a leader among men, holding the room with his conviction.

By the eighth hour, the two stable hands returned. Robert rose to meet them and hear their reports. From the shake of their heads and the shadow that passed across my son's face, it was clear the response had been poor.

A silence settled on the company.

It was only for a moment that Robert wavered but then he raised himself upright once more. "My friends, we must away. We are expected and we should not keep our companions waiting."

The company rose and donned cloaks, gloves and hats.

At the gates, fresh horses had been readied, with supplies for the next stage of their journey.

As Robert prepared to mount his horse, I drew close to him. "May God speed you and protect you, my son. Be careful."

He turned and pulled me into an embrace. "I will, as far as I am able. I will return as soon as it is safe to do so."

His words, I knew then, were borne of hope rather than true expectation. The hope burned bright but its foundations were not as solid as he believed.

They mounted their horses and departed from the gatehouse.

I stood in the cold night air, watching my son, illuminated by lantern light, diminish as he rode down the lane with his companions.

It was the last sight I ever had of him.

The next day, he led a raid on Warwick Castle to take weapons and horses for an uprising that never came to be.

Two days after that, the eighth of November, 1605, he was shot by musket fire as his companions made a stand at Holbeche House on the Staffordshire border. The executions of those who survived were deliberately cruel. My son was fortunate to have the swift death that he did.

The Devil's Work

Kristian Longden

July, 1612. A jeering crowd, a child crying. My child, or another's? Chains clinking, the soft thud of boots on wood. Rope squeezing flesh. Throats gargling, gasping, begging for air. Cracking bones. The flutter of birds.

Then, much louder, a fast, urgent pounding. A fist beating against a door. It became my world, devouring all else. The sound was rushing closer, surging through the darkness.

For me? Was it coming for me?

I started from my pillow sweating, 'though the night was a bitter chill. For a moment, I simply lay there, dazed and confused. I was sure I had been dreaming until that godless banging started at my door again. It hammered through the house like a hawker on market day. I pressed my temples. My skull was near to splitting, my tongue rank with the taste of smoke and brandywine from the previous evening.

The children would be awake by now. As if in answer, the cries of two babes joined the chorus.

"Mr Ashcombe?" came a worried whisper from

outside my bedchamber.

"Yes, Hannah, I'm awake," I groaned. "What in God's holy name is going on?"

"It's the constable. He is making quite the disturbance, sir, the children are awake and – "

"I can hear it well enough," I snapped, rising from my bed. "You had better let him in. Sit him in the parlour. Two cups of wine, please, Hannah. And bring the jug. Then calm the children. I will be down in a moment."

Dutifully, Hannah shuffled off.

I pulled back the curtain to glance out of the window. The sky was inky black. To call on me at this hour and in this fashion surely marked dark tidings. Indeed, it had been many months since my old friend had come to me for business or for fellowship.

I reached for the bottle of brandywine hidden beneath my desk and took a deep, restorative draught.

"Give me strength, Hester," I murmured wearily, fingering the ring I kept by my parchments.

It had been my wife's favourite, a silver band set with tiny rubies, a subtle "H" graven upon the signet. I pressed the ring against my lips before carefully returning it to its place. I sighed, dressed and descended the stairs to see what fate awaited me.

Hannah had done what she could to make the house welcoming on such short notice. Several candles had been lit, that our meeting might not be held in total darkness, and the scent of juniper hung pleasantly in the air.

Upon entering the parlour, I found Henry Wentworth slouched low in his chair, hands playing restlessly in his lap, his winecup already drained.

"Henry," I greeted the constable, making no effort to conceal the irritation in my voice. "You gave the house quite a fright, clattering about at this hour." I took the flagon of wine and refilled his cup, then pulled up a chair to sit opposite him.

"Simon," he said, pushing himself upright. By the way he struggled, I could tell the constable was drunk. "It has been too long, my friend. You look well."

The same could not be said for him. In truth, the man before me bore little resemblance to the Wentworth I recalled from mere months past. That Wentworth had worn a thick brush of jet black hair, was built like an ox and never unpopular with the genteel ladies. Now his pate was thin and speckled with white; nose and cheekbones stood out gaunt and angular; his eyes were wet and glassy; the scent on his breath was vile and acrid.

"I am as well as I can be, all considered." I took a well-needed gulp of wine, eager to reach the root of this business. Besides, I wished not to dwell on personal affairs, his nor mine. Not at this hour, not after his dramatics and certainly not while he was swilled and stinking like a sow.

"Let us," I continued coldly, "skip the pleasantries tonight, Henry, if you would not mind. If you would care to share what it is that necessitates that you scare my maid half to death, wake my infant children and drag me from my bed."

My tone must have taken him by surprise.

The man looked close to tears. He dropped his head to stare at the floor.

A flush of anger rose over me as I contemplated whether this was naught more than a drunken fool's misadventure.

Then it was my turn to be surprised.

"Miles Thorpe is dead," murmured Wentworth. "I found him earlier this night, hanging by the neck."

"A self-murder?"

"He owed me coin. I had emptied my purse at Alice's, down in The Drapery, and thought to go and collect – "

I noted Wentworth wasn't answering my question directly.

" – my debt. God, you should have smelled him, Simon. Emptied my entire stomach right there on the floor. And his – "

To my horror, Wentworth was trembling.

"Steady, man," I urged him. "Did you call for the coroner?"

Wentworth scrunched his eyes and clenched his fists. In an act that seemed to cause him great pain, he shook his head.

I could only gape at him. Sad and shocking as the news of Miles's death was, it paled in comparison to the wretched state of the man before me.

"You are a constable of Northampton, for God's sake!" I chided. "Your calling has made you no stranger to a corpse. Why run howling to me rather than call for the coroner?"

Wentworth snapped his head up to glare at me. There was a madness to his eyes that I did not like. It spoke to both fear and frenzy.

"Neither of us are strangers to corpses now, are we, my friend? *That* is the reason I came to you."

He spat these words with such venom I thought he might strike me. Then he threw back his head to empty his wine cup a second time, wiping his mouth on his sleeve when he was sated.

"Let me be clearer," he slurred, "on the condition in which I discovered Miles. He was swinging above a rancid pool of his own putrefied flesh. The flies had made a fine home of what little remained of him, their young writhing in his belly, plump as geese in Christmastide."

As Wentworth lurched towards me, I fell back into my chair. His fingers dug painfully into my shoulders as he seized me, his face just inches from my own.

"Now mark this," he hissed, spraying me with spittle. "I had seen him earlier that very day, supping at Alice's. So tell me, Simon, ought I have summoned the coroner? Or come to an old friend who I thought might grasp the kind of danger we face here?"

To my relief, Wentworth let me go. Abandoning all courtesy, he poured himself another cup of wine.

Shaking, I reached for my own and gulped it down, praying it might bring some respite to this grotesque exhibition. I watched Wentworth sit down and stare absently at the tapestry of Northampton Castle, the centrepiece of the room. Despite his behaviour, I felt a drop of pity for him. The deep shadows under his eyes spoke of a man who had not slept much of late. They were a stark contrast to the sickly cast of his cheeks.

"Go home and get some rest," I suggested, not unkindly. "And first thing, fetch the coroner so that poor Miles might be spared further indignity."

"You do not believe me," Wentworth sighed wearily.

"I believe you are blind drunk and, by the looks of it, an ill man. I believe you have suffered quite the shock this night, which is why I have already forgiven you for this evening's mishap."

Though it pained me, I stood firm as Wentworth's mouth quivered, the wound of betrayal evident on his face.

"I shall take my leave then," he scowled, stumbling to the doorway.

I followed him through the gloom of the house and watched as he wandered through the garden out into the darkness. Before disappearing, he turned – as though to say one more thing – then thought the better of it and carried on his way.

When I was certain Wentworth was gone, I returned inside and immediately sought out the pantry for a fresh jug of wine. No – brandywine would be needed tonight. I fetched that from the cupboard instead and sat down to reckon with the events of the evening.

I strove not to dwell on Miles's self-murder. The manner of his death struck too near certain chapters of my own life.

Yet I would mourn him, for he had been instrumental in our efforts to purge Northampton of witchery. It was Miles who observed and recorded, who passed the information to myself and Wentworth so we could gather testimonies and pen depositions.

What had driven him to that desperate end I could not guess, for I had not seen the man since our business was concluded. But I had heard rumour that he, like Wentworth, had since grown fond of the grape.

As for Wentworth? What he claimed was sick and preposterous. What he implied to have been witchcraft was the fevered rambling of a man galloping the same road as Miles. His tale was untrue of anything we knew to be true of the black magic. Witchery was subtle. Fresh milk going sour in the pail. Bread that would not rise, no matter the kneading. Well-bred livestock producing stillborn calves. All rumour and mutterings: hearsay until one makes the connections.

I decided that, on the morrow, I would fetch the coroner myself. I had doubts that Wentworth would even recall what had transpired this night and I did not trust he would be in a fit state to perform his duty.

Then I would seek out Sir Montagu at the Castle

to see what could be done for Wentworth. For all his decline, the man had diligently served both the people and the Crown during the witch trials and I hoped that Montagu could arrange some manner of help for him.

With a solid plan in mind, I resolved to relax and savour the fine brandywine. Imported from the Dutch Republic, it was smooth and warm on the throat and did wonders to dull the senses and quiet the mind for a sound night's sleep.

I was lost in thoughts when Hannah peered in around the door. "Mr Ashcombe? Are you well?"

I caught her eyes flicker to the empty glass at my side before returning to meet mine.

"Very well, thank you, Hannah. Come in, sit down. Have a drink with me."

"It is late, sir. Morning can't be far off. Perhaps it is best to get some sleep?"

"How dull," I drawled. "There is little point in sleeping now, is there? Fetch us some wine and join me."

Hannah tiptoed inside and gently closed the door. Always thinking of the children. "It smells like a whorehouse in here," she grumbled, hurrying over to the window, throwing it wide to let the chill air seep in.

"By Jesu!" I exclaimed. "Shut that before I catch the death of cold."

Hannah turned and scowled at me. "Absolutely not. I shall be in here with Edith and Martha in a few short hours and I will not have it smelling of debauchery. They may be babes, Mr Ashcombe, but such things will leave a mark on them."

There was naught I could do but sulk in my chair. I knew most would be horrified to see a maid speak so to her employer but, without Hannah, I would be lost. I had grown accustomed to her impertinence, for more often than not, she spoke the truth of it.

"May I speak plain?" she said.

"And what was that, if not plain?" I said, laughing in spite of myself.

Hannah did not return to humour. "I have been in your service almost a year, Mr Ashcombe. In that time, I have – " She looked away, failing to hide the tears that collected in her eyes. "And in that time," she sighed, "I have grown to love your children as my own."

"As I hoped you would," I said.

"Forgive my bluntness, sir, but believe me when I say that I speak honestly. Edith and Martha deserve better. Nay, they *need* better. This drink… so many late nights… always seeking solitude in your study… you are withholding from them a father they still have. When was the last time you held them? Most days you do not so much as visit, though we live under the same roof! I know the grief you have held since your wife's passing but, I beg of you, do not orphan them in all but name."

Each awful word she uttered struck me like a dart. The seed of despair I held ever-present in my chest began to bloom, growing gnarled branches that I thought might pierce straight through my heart. But then a heat rose within me, a wave of fire to burn it all away.

"*OUT!*" I bellowed, rising with such fury that I almost stumbled to the floor. God above, I was swilled. "Remember your place, Hannah. You are a maidservant, naught more. It is not, and never shall be, your place to chastise me so. Perhaps stroll to the villages tomorrow and see how the peasant folk live – in shit and squalor. Then return and judge the conditions in which I raise my children."

To her credit, Hannah did not cower. "Mr Ashcombe, I – "

"I will not hear another word of it!" I fought against the urge to take the empty bottle of brandy and slam down on her skull. Instead, I thrust a shaking finger toward the door. "Out," I repeated, dismissing her like a disobedient bitch.

Hannah must have grasped the finality of my words. She took a long look at me, her face a bitter knot of disgust, pity, and contempt. Then, as bid, she left me to my seething.

Once alone, I let out a long, rasping sigh. It seemed as though I had been too lax with Hannah, after all. She had always had a sharp tongue, often overreaching the line of what was expected from a woman of her station. But I had always overlooked it, for her spirit was a soothing balm to this cursed and joyless household and her unwavering devotion to

Edith and Martha had never faltered.

Yet tonight, Hannah had overstepped. If she dared to speak so uncouthly again, she would be dismissed without hesitation. Order would need to be restored, expectations set plain. I added this to the actions I would take on the morrow. Visit the coroner, speak with Montagu and chastise Hannah in regard to her conduct.

Now, I decided, it was time for bed. I pulled in the window Hannah opened earlier, marking the deep navy hue to the sky. Dawn would arrive soon. Wearied in body and soul, I climbed the stairs.

On my way to my bedchamber, I resolved to look at the children. Gently, I pushed open the door to the back room where Edith and Martha slept. They looked so peaceful, so small, deep within the realms of slumber.

Edith lay on her back, head tilted to the right, one tiny hand curled at her chin. Next to her, Martha slept with her mouth slightly open, her breath soft and steady.

For a moment, I simply watched, the anger in me softening, the whirring thoughts settling. I allowed the tears to fall. They streaked my face like rainwater on a windowpane, warm against the cold of my cheeks. In several ways, tonight's events had reopened a chapter of my life that I often prayed was behind me.

It had been the King's work, nay, God's work: righteous, necessary, but foul. Wentworth, Miles and I had spent many months putting together the evidence under the close watch of Sir Montagu.

We strove to keep our work a secret, but it was not long before folk gave me a wide berth or averted their eyes to the gutter as I passed them in the streets. Strangers came to know my face and many friends turned to strangers in those months. Yet I pressed on, for there was no other choice.

That rain-soaked day at Abington gallows, when we gathered to watch the accursed hang, was painful. Both Wentworth and I had pleaded to Montagu for more time. The evidence compiled could hardly be considered conclusive. It was enough to demand a trial, but was it enough to damn a soul to eternal torment?

But Montagu was insistent. "The King demands it," he had said.

The words brooked no further discussion.

Five stood there atop the gallows. Weeping, cursing, begging. Professing their innocence. Arthur Bill of Raunds. Mary Barber of Stanwick. Agnes Browne of Guilsborough. Her daughter, Joan. And of course, Helen Jenkinson of Thrapston.

Helen, the sister of my dear wife.

Hester, my wife, did not attend her sister's hanging. It was the only small mercy I could grant her. She remained at the house with Edith and Martha, who were but weeks old at the time. I returned after the execution to find that Hester had locked herself away with the babes, the bedchamber door barred from within. Through the wood she inflicted the devil's own wrath upon me, shrieking, wailing and cursing me for all I was worth. She swore she would rather take herself and the children from this cruel world than allow me to enter.

By some miracle, God gave me the words to talk her down and out of it. But nothing was the same after that day. She would converse with me only in silent gestures or bare replies. I cannot recall her ever again mothering our children.

Several miserable weeks went by before Hester kept to half the promise she had made on that fateful day. Nothing in life prepares you for the impossibility of coming home to find your beloved wife's wrists slashed to bloody ruin, nor for learning the wounds were of her own making. How angry I had been at her for abandoning her husband and infant daughters through an act of such egregious sin, and furious at God for permitting her to do so.

Infants though my daughters are, I am confident they feel the absence of their mother's tender grace so cruelly snatched from them. While sustenance and gentle tones provided by Hannah have done some to calm their spirits, I still cannot shake the dreadful sense that the innocence of these two gentle souls will be forever broken by their mother's ruin.

I composed myself and wiped away the tears. Sleep was long overdue. Quietly, I slipped from the bedside and crept down the hall to my own bed. I collapsed into it to drift towards a restless, uneasy sleep.

I rose mid-morning, later than I would have liked,

but understandable given the circumstances. Before departing, I exchanged a few curt words with Hannah, if only to inform her that I would likely be gone until the afternoon.

"I should like a word with you when I return," I added on my way out.

"As you say, sir," she said, her tone as cold as the morning air.

The coroner's office was in St Peter's at the other side of town. Despite the lateness of the hour, today was the Sabbath and Northampton's streets were relatively empty. I made my way south through an empty Sheep Market and across Marhold Square. The fresh air was doing much for my spirits. It had been so long since I had been out and about the town.

My thoughts wandered to Wentworth and the events of the night before. With a change of heart, I decided to detour and check if Wentworth had already spoken to the coroner that morning. I doubted it but wanted to give him another chance to do so. I feared how poorly it would reflect on him if the coroner were to learn of the matter from me or suspect Wentworth had delayed reporting the death.

I needed not enter Wentworth's house to know something was ghastly amiss. As I went to knock, the stench assailed my nostrils so violently that I collapsed there on his threshold to retch. Vomit poured out of me, pooling at my knees and drenching my coat.

When the tremors stopped, I wiped my mouth and

edged inside, dreading what I might find. The unspeakable scent of rot and corruption was so unbearable I thought I might faint. I tiptoed through the silent house, my heart swelling against my ribcage, my breath frozen in my throat.

I found what was left of Henry Wentworth swinging by the hearth. Flies had already made a nest of him, burrowing deep into the meagre scraps of flesh that still clung to his yellowing bones. Rank fluids oozed from his carcass, soaking the fur rug beneath and tinting it a sickly green.

And yet – despite the sheer incredulity of what hung truly there before me – my eyes moved to a skeletal finger on Wentworth's right hand. There, unmistakable, even beneath a smearing of putrid gore, rested a silver ring set with rubies.

The signet was etched with a single letter: H.

My thoughts shattered into shards of impossibility, each crashed together, waging war inside my skull. That corpse could not exist. I had sent its owner cursing from my house only hours before. And that ring could not be on that finger, for I had held it in my hand – pressed it against my own lips – that same night.

I fled, forgetting the ring, fearing to linger even a moment more might cause irreparable damage to my fractured mind.

I tore from that wretched house into the street. Any folk who witnessed me hurrying homeward through the town must have thought me sick and rabid. But I paid them no mind.

As I raced home, despite all I had just witnessed, I was obsessed with one thing: Hester's ring.

Deep within the recess of my mind, where a frail thread of sanity still barely clung, I tried to make sense of it. Wentworth was no thief and, besides, I had not once left his side when he had visited me. He was given no opportunity to sneak upstairs to my bedchamber and steal it.

Could it have been Hannah? Surely not. Yet I saw no alternative, for she had remained upstairs throughout our entire conversation.

Had she secretly been Wentworth's lover? Had she taken pity on him after hearing how I chastised him and, in some spiteful gesture, tossed him the ring out of the window once he had left?

Such a jewel could fetch a pretty penny, could fund more of his lecherous nights at Alice's. I had gone straight to fetch the brandywine and returned to the parlour, after all. It would not have been difficult for Hannah to steal the ring and throw it down to Wentworth.

"Hannah!" I roared, bursting into my home like a rampaging ox. "Show your face at once, thief!"

I looked down the hallway through to the kitchen and caught Hannah eying me with terror and confusion. Quicker than I had any right to be, I charged and in two heartbeats was upon her, clutching her by the throat, slamming her against the wall. The force shook the room so violently that pots and pans clattered to the floor.

"Why?" I demanded. "Why would you betray me so?"

Behind us, the children were screaming.

"Speak, or I swear on God's name, I will kill you."

I loosened my grip enough for her to choke out a response. "I don't understand," she gasped between gargled breaths.

"And now you deny it!" I spat furiously. "Did you think I would not find out? That the absence of my most prized possession would go unnoticed?"

Hannah gawped at me dumbly.

"The ring, damn it. I know you stole my wife's ring!"

Though her eyes remained wide with fright, her body relaxed somewhat. "Mr Ashcombe, the ring is upstairs. I polished it this very morning."

"Impossible," I spluttered. I removed my hands from Hannah's throat. Bruises were already blooming on the pale of her neck.

Without another word, I abandoned my injured maid and the wailing children and ran upstairs.

The ring was there, of course. Right where it should have been.

Had I dreamt it? Had Wentworth's midnight call and Hannah's ugly words plagued me with an all too real bout of night terrors? The thought gave me a momentary wave of respite until I looked down to see my vomit-stained tunic.

I had hallucinated then, surely. The shock of

discovering an old friend, the victim of his own self-murder, had conjured visions of things that were not there. I was sure that if I notified the coroner and listened to his findings, he would conclude nothing more than a blasphemous deed had taken place and confirm that the state in which I found him – and the sight of that ring – were but the twisted fabrications of a mind pushed well beyond its limits.

I was almost relieved were it not for an unplaceable feeling of terror that wormed its way through my chest. It bored its way through me until I could not ignore the root of it.

The realisation overcame me.

Helen – my wife's sister, the damned witch of her family – had worn a selfsame ring.

Their mother, always fond of their shared initial and fonder still of her daughters, had commissioned a jeweller to craft matching bands to celebrate their sisterhood.

But we had *buried* Helen with that ring.

It remains my most shameful secret although, at the time, I thought a better burial might restore some humanity to Hester. It is forbidden to bury on sacred ground those condemned as witches. Helen and the others were to be thrown in unmarked graves by the gallows.

I knew the day they were to be cut down. On that morning, I spoke with the gravedigger, claiming I had been given permission to bury Helen in the woods behind our home and that we hoped in placing her close family, her damned spirit might find peace. The badge that has marked me as official was enough for the gravedigger. Nodding at me to take her, he loaded her swaddled corpse on to my cart.

And so we buried her, along with some of her prize trinkets in the hope they might grant a sliver of mercy to her soul.

I hurried downstairs to Hannah who was standing there, soothing the children while nursing her neck with a wet cloth.

"The dead have risen!" I cried.

"Mr Ashcombe, you are a sick man!" she screamed, bursting into tears. "Leave us, I beg you! Leave us and find help for the sickness that has poisoned your mind!"

I stooped to retrieve the heavy iron pot I had knocked from the stove during our earlier altercation. With all my might, I hurled it across the room. Hannah shrieked and, with remarkable speed, ducked out of the way. I winced as it struck the floor with a deafening crash, mere inches from where Edith sat bawling.

Resolved to prove my impossible theory, I hurried outside to fetch the shovel. I spent the remaining daylight hours in the forest at the rear of the house, digging frantically, certain I would find no corpse there. The heavens must have opened for, as night drew close, the soil turned to mud. Toiling through the sucking mire, I reached a most ghastly conclusion.

It was clear as day to me, now, that Helen had

returned to deliver vengeance to those who had conspired in her condemnation. In so doing, she marked her victims with the putrid scar of witchery.

It was close to midnight by the time I was satisfied the business was concluded. The light of a gibbous moon exposed the excavated ground around me, empty graves all.

I shambled back to the house, dragging my shovel through the mire, ready with instructions for Hannah to ready the babes for travel at once. We would leave this place tonight, flee this unholy ground in hope that our souls may yet be saved.

But when I arrived home, the house was dark, cold and empty. I tracked mud through the house as I searched each room thrice over, calling all the while. The only response I received was from the demons thrashing around in my head. Laughing to myself, I opened the wardrobes in the children's bedchamber to find some items missing. Not many, but enough for a few days' travel at least.

The foolish woman would pay for this. With the help of Sir Montagu, it would not take long for us to track her down. I would go to him first thing in the morning and together we would set things right.

Pleased with this plan, I wandered into the pantry for some more brandywine. Liquid gold, sweet nectar.

I made for the parlour. It was good to sink into the chair after such a laborious day.

Eager to numb my sorrows, I guzzled greedily, desperately. Though the liquor burned in my throat, it did nothing to warm the soul. I lay back and giggled, realising no mercy would be found drinking tonight.

Not this night nor the next.

I unclasped my belt, setting it neatly on the table beside me. It was worn out travelling leather, ragged and fraying with age and use.

Strong enough, though. Strong enough.

It had served me well for many years.

And I suspected it would serve me well once again this night.

By Now, Darkness Has Fallen
Michael J Richards

To get from Creaton – a small village north-west of Northampton – to Guilsborough, a little more north-west – you take the Hollowell Road for about half a mile. At that random point, it changes its name to Creaton Road, which takes you into Hollowell.

Coming out of Hollowell, the road changes its name again, this time to Guilsborough Road. Physically, it's the same road from Creaton to Guilsborough but, depending on where you are, its identity is different.

The journey from Creaton to Guilsborough is about two and a half miles. So, on a bright spring morning or a rusty autumn evening, it's a lovely walk. At an average walking speed of four miles an hour, that's about forty minutes. If it's a leisurely stroll, enjoying deliciously clean air and gorgeous nature, then it's maybe fifty.

The road is wide enough, in places, for two cars. Bordering each side are high bushes, medium height hawthorn hedgerows and tall trees which mark the boundaries of neighbouring fields.

It's likely the hedgerows along this road were planted about 1740, following the Bills of Enclosure which started in 1603. It's also likely that those hedgerows are the hedgerows we see today.

If you think about it, the only difference between the Creaton Road of today and that of, say, the mid-1760s, is the surface. Unlike now, it would have been natural surfacing – mud, dust, grass, weeds – all worn down, and kept down, by carts, wagons, coaches, human and animal tread.

Creaton Road
between Creaton and Hollowell,
Northamptonshire
Wednesday, 28 September 1763

Autumn begins. Sunset comes earlier.

By the time Gabriel Adams has finished his day's work and had a meal – about eight in the evening – it's already dark.

He's put his coat and hat on. He's well on his way along Creaton Road towards Hollowell and then Guilsborough. It's dark enough so that, if he didn't already know his way, he'd be falling into roadside ditches or getting his face scratched by overhanging hawthorn.

Gabriel is in love. Today, although Jessica doesn't know it yet, he's on his way to her home in Guilsborough to propose marriage. He fell in love with her the moment he first saw her. Unfortunately, that moment was at her husband's funeral two years ago.

Michael died by drowning, trying to rescue Stevie, his setter, from a well. John Bateman, his employer, the local magistrate and squire, had insisted on paying for the funeral.

Gabriel knew Michael but, until that time, hadn't met Jessica, his wife, now his widow. But when he first saw her, he knew he had to wait a decent time before commencing courtship.

He's lonely. Rachel, his own wife, died in childbirth four years ago. He needs a woman by his side. Jessica, a yarn spinner, with Harold and Gretchen, her two children, is the perfect choice. Louis, his own six-year-old son, is healthy and intelligent.

Gabriel's on a good income. He's 31, is in full health with a fit, muscular body – he's the village blacksmith – with a comfortable home, big enough for what will become, he hopes, his new family – a wife and three children. He's earning about eight shillings a day. He and Jessica can afford to keep them all.

As he walks along, humming love songs, he pats his coat pockets. In one, engagement and wedding rings, both of which he's made. In another, some pennies for the children and a small, decorated metal box – which he's also made and will give to Jessica as a –

"Hullo, friend."

Gabriel stops. The voice comes from a few yards ahead. He can't see anyone.

"I said, hullo, friend."

Approaching footsteps scrunch on stones.

Seconds later, someone's face appears so close that Gabriel can't step aside without pushing him away. He doesn't want to come into contact with the stranger. That always ends badly. He sees a big hat down over the stranger's eyes. A thick, black scarf covers his nose and mouth.

"Give me everything you got in your pockets."

"No."

The stranger slams Gabriel on the side of his head.

"Give me everything you got in your pockets."

But Gabriel doesn't hear him too well this time. His ear hurting, he's staggering, trying to retain his balance.

"Here, friend," a different voice, a deeper voice, says behind him, "let me help you."

Two arms catch him, stand him up.

When Gabriel is steady and balanced, he feels hands go into his pockets, pulling out the rings, the coins and the box.

"What you found?" It's a third voice, higher than the others. "Any good?"

"Take 'em."

"Move aside." This is a fourth voice.

Gabriel can't work out how many there are.

All men. Obviously.

Footpads. Probably.

A gang. Clearly.

Another two hands pull away the arms that were supporting him. Those new hands grab hold of Gabriel's coat collar, pulls it down over his back. Other hands, a pair for each arm, wrench the sleeves over his knuckles. The coat is off.

"Nice material, lads."

Gabriel sees shadows, outlines, silhouettes playing with his coat.

"Yeah. That'll fetch a few shillings."

"The shirt, the shirt. Get the shirt."

The work of a minute.

His long shirt is off.

This being late September, he now feels cold. He shivers.

"Are the trousers any good?"

One of them kneels, his hands running up and down Gabriel's thighs and shins. "Ain't worth it," he growls.

"What about the boots?"

"Nah," the one with the high voice grunts, feeling Gabriel's feet. "Too much trouble, not worth the effort."

"That's it, then. C'm' on, boys, let's be off."

Catslo House, the home of Thomas Seamark
Guilsborough
Tuesday, 18 October 1763
20 days later

"So what we got, Tom?"

Tom is Thomas Seamark, 32, married to Ann, a seamstress from Cottesbrooke. Three children.

He's a tall, thin fellow who likes to model himself on a tattered picture of Charles I he has somewhere in a drawer – sharp, chestnut brown moustache pointed up at the ends; a small, carefully combed beard in the centre of the chin; long, auburn curls nearly touching his shoulders.

Catslo House, where they live, has two bedrooms, a kitchen with a large table, six chairs and a modern oven – it has front doors. Seamark keeps dogs and pigs at the back. A mile outside Guilsborough, he owns a field where he keeps his horse.

He has no visible occupation or financial support. While everyone in the village knows he's a professional highwayman, the law has little or no evidence to arrest him.

"So what we got, Tom?"

"Well, John," Seamark says, opening a large chest.

John Croxford, 23, a tailor. Medium height, thinner than Seamark. Untidy, uncared for. Probably hasn't washed in a week. Croxford was born in Brixworth of respectable parents who ensured he received a liberal education, which he has wasted. He likes to associate with gamblers, thieves, loose women. He has a permanent air of disappointment that, at his age, he is still unmarried.

He pulls out a finely made coat, a silk shirt, a linen shirt, two silk scarves, a metal box, coins, banknotes, rings, other jewellery, other assorted trinkets, purses, pipes.

"A fine collection," Croxford says, fingering the jewellery. "We've done well."

"That we have," Seamark says. "Ben, what's your fancy?"

"I have my eyes on the coat."

"Then, my good friend," Seamark says, "it is yours."

Benjamin Deacon, 25, married with two children. Born in Spratton, a village some four miles away. A thatch of dark blond hair which he never combs – he thinks of it as a style, 'though it's probably more to do with laziness – he's still trying to grow a moustache, getting nowhere with it. Employed as a sawyer in a sawmill in Harlestone, some eleven miles away, he hates his work, is always looking for something else, has a profound, unending interest in beer and thieving.

He stands up, puts the coat on. "Hey," he says, walking up and down the kitchen, "isn't this the coat we purloined along the Creaton Road a couple of weeks ago?"

"You're right," Butlin, the fourth member of the gang says. "Methought I recognised it. 'Tis a fine garment. It fits you well."

Richard Butlin, 20, a glover and breeches maker. Rotund and, even at his age, starting to lose his hair, he's popular in the village, born of well-bred Guilsborough parentage who gave him a good education. A friendly chap who wishes no ill-will towards anyone, except those who get in the way of his childish, sociopathic need to snatch fine clothes and fancy trinkets from people who can afford them. Even then, he is always polite while lifting goods from their persons and even politer when he's slapping them about.

A knock-knock-knocking at the door.

Without a word, the four pile the stuff back into the chest, push the chest under the table, sit casually.

"Scottie," Seamark says, opening the door. "Come in. Good to see you. What do you have for us to see?"

"Scottie" is Thomas Corey, a travelling pedlar, a lithe, sprightly, balding 43-year-old who spends his days walking from Northamptonshire village to Northamptonshire village buying cheaply from craftsmen and women, selling at good profits, eating what he can get, sleeping where he can.

"I'm obliged to you, Master Seamark," he says, carrying his basket in. "I've some fine things to show you. Of that I'm sure."

He rests his walking-stick against the table, drops the basket on the floor, bends down, pulls out a turquoise silk scarf.

"One of you fine, honest, handsome gentlemen," he says, standing up, "will approve of this, I'm confident. I'm also confident you'll please your beautiful lady when you present her with – "

He looks around. Not a glimmer of interest.

He brings out a bracelet decorated with miniature gargoyle faces, carved from oak.

"Something for an attractive young maiden, I think."

No-one moves.

"Very well," he says, putting it away, refusing to be discouraged, pulling out a pair of men's stockings, spreading them over his forearms. "A sumptuous pair of ribbed cotton stockings in maroon and white stripes. For every well-dressed man about town." He walks around the room, pausing before each man.

"Man about town?" Seamark says. "We're in Guilsborough, not your fancy London gambling dives."

"Stockings?" Deacon sneers. "Do I look like someone who'd wear stockings?"

"Sling yer 'ook, mate," Croxford says. "Clear off."

"As you wish," Scottie chuckles. He puts the stockings away, picks up the basket and his stick. "Maybe next time," he says, turning towards them, "I'll have something to please you. Maybe next time." He edges his basket out, closes the door.

The four men settle around the table, drink their ale.

"An acceptable fellow," Deacon says, slapping his mug down. "'Tis a pity he had nothing for us."

"'T ain't a pity at all," Butlin grumps. "Stockings. Does he think we're a stable of mollies? If I had my way, I'd beat him all the way to Araby and back."

"You're right, Croxford says. "Let's get him, let's

do him in." He looks around the table. "Everyone up for it?"

"I'm in," Seamark says.

"If you are, then so am I," Butlin nods, smiling straight at him.

"Me, too," Deacon says.

It doesn't take them long to find Scottie. In the few minutes since he left them, he hasn't got far, only a few yards to Seamark's neighbour, who bought the stockings Deacon was insulted by, and a few dozen footsteps after that.

Surrounded by the four of them, Scottie doesn't stand a chance. They drag him along, his feet catching in the dusty, stone-cracked street –

"What is it, gentlemen," he wails, "that has caused you offence? In what manner have I slighted you? Tell me, I beg you. I promise to put it right."

– and throw him into Seamark's scrub of a garden at the back of Catslo House. He falls against a wilting shrub, stands up, goes towards them.

"What is it that I have done that causes you so much anger?"

"Keep your gob shut," Seamark snarls, stepping towards him.

His right fist clenched hard, he lunges. As his knuckles smash into Scottie's jaw, he hears cracking teeth. Scottie stumbles backwards, falls down, his hands clutching his mouth, his body hitting the shrub and then the ground, his ankles twisting as he lands, his scream muffled, his eyes popping in disbelief.

Scarlet blood crawls through his fingers, more blood and yellowing snot shoot from his nose.

No sooner is he down, Butlin is kneeling on his legs. Deacon, sitting on his face, is bouncing up and down, giggling like a bullying child suffocating the black cat of a wrongly accused witch.

"Let's get him indoors," Seamark whispers. "Safer indoors."

Butlin gets up. Deacon calms down.

Each grabs a shoulder or leg. They drag him into the kitchen and hoist him on to the table. His head settles there. His ankles and feet dangle over the other end.

"What do we do now?" Deacon spits.

Croxford has a wooden carving knife. He took it from a carpenter a few months ago along the Teeton Road. He leans over the pedlar, takes the knife from his pocket, cuts the pedlar's throat. Not a simple, light slitting. But deep into the gullet, deep through the vocal chords, deep to the back of the neck. Blood spills out, sideways, pouring away like ale spilled from a Toby Jug tankard. The head is almost off. But not quite. The body jerks, spasms, jumps.

"Aaah," Croxford groans as if in orgasmic ecstasy, stabbing him in the head again and again – altogether, five times. He brings himself up, sweat drooling down his face, his grubby shirt soaked, his hands blood-red-drenched.

"That's it," he chortles, stepping away, laughing. "Got him good and proper."

A breathless Croxford is at the sink. He's taken off his shirt and is washing himself, clearing the blood from his skin. Deacon and Butlin stand back, slack-jawed, grim-faced, eyes half-closed.

Seamark, who has done nothing so far, comes forward. As Deacon and Butlin watch, he strips the dead body. Finds a small, cloth money bag in a trouser pocket, puts it to one side.

After Seamark has removed Scottie's linen drawers, Deacon and Butlin — without a word, no-one speaks — fold the clothes. Seamark takes the garments upstairs into the children's bedroom, they're asleep, puts them in a blanket box. When he comes back down, Croxford and the others are staring at the head hanging from the neck of the naked corpse.

"Right, lads," he says, "now we bury the snivelling lobcock."

"Where's Mrs Seamark?" Deacon says.

"What?"

"Where's your wife?"

"Oh, I understand," Seamark says. "Northampton for a few days, selling her clothwork."

By now, darkness has fallen. Seamark lights a lantern, goes out the back to a small shed. He brings out four shovels, hands them out.

"Over there," he whispers, pointing to a small piece of land beyond the house.

Generally speaking, it takes about five hours for a practised gravedigger to dig a six-foot grave. Here, the soil is soft, easy, so, with the four of them — two working, two resting – it takes nearly four hours. By midnight, they're finished.

Seamark finds an old bedsheet hanging about in the shed. They take it into the kitchen, wrap the naked pedlar in it, carry the bundle out, drop it into the sunken grave. It takes the four men half an hour to shovel the soil back. The surplus is smoothed over the land. They go back indoors, drink some ale, have a smoke. Nothing is said. They have nothing to say. They're tired, dazed, puzzled.

After twenty minutes' silence, Seamark says, "We'll stay together until dawn. Then, we'll make sure everything is cleared away and clean before we separate. Richard, Ben, you shall sleep in our bed upstairs in the room next to the children. John, we've comfortable armchairs in the parlour. We'll sleep there.

"When you use the privy, be as quiet as you can. Most of all, my friends, make sure you're not seen. I don't want the children knowing anything about this. I'll fetch you after they're away at school. Stay in your rooms 'til I fetch you."

A few minutes after six next morning, sunrise, Seamark frees the dogs from their kennels. It doesn't take them long to find Scottie's grave. They're pawing, snuffling, scuffling at the soil in no time. Also, and in no time, Seamark scurries about, putting them back, tying them up, in their kennels. They bark their heads off for the next ten minutes, scratching to be let loose, then give up.

An hour later, the children – Jed, Toby, Claudia – are off, Claudia and Jed to Gilbert's Writing School, Toby to the endowed Grammar School, all for a 7.30 start. They'll be back at two, ready to work, cleaning the house, walking the dogs, feeding the pigs, helping neighbours.

"No good, lads," Seamark says, handing out bread and milk. "We've got to dig Scottie up, dispose of him some other way."

After they've eaten, it doesn't take long to get him out of the earthen grave. As the soil is already disturbed from last night's burial, an hour at the most.

They drag Scottie back into the kitchen, unwrap him. While Croxford, Deacon and Butlin are laying him on the table, Seamark fetches a couple of saws and buckets from the shed. Seamark and Croxford cut him up – the head is already dangling from the neck so that's easy. Butlin and Deacon wipe up the blood and other body parts to make sure the place is kept clean.

The head, arms, hands, legs, feet and flesh of the torso are pushed into the oven and, while they're cooking, the rest of the body – the remains of the flesh, organs, entrails, blood – are fed to the pigs and dogs. It's a lot for the animals to gobble up but, within a couple of hours, they've done it.

The men use hammers to smash the bones into dust and fragments. They bury them back in the garden. The cooked meat is taken from the oven and thrown to the pigs. They burn his basket and wares, bury the ashes.

Seamark empties the money bag. £1 2s 4½d in coins. Seamark keeps 7s 4½d for himself, gives the others 5s each. After that, everything that was Scottie has truly gone.

Early afternoon, the children tumble into the house, have bread and cheese, are out again, attending to their duties. Mrs Seamark arrives home early evening.

Catslo House, the home of Thomas Seamark
Guilsborough
Sunday, 23 October 1763
3 days later

Sundays at the Seamark home are usually spent attending St Etheldreda's in the morning, roast dinner – Seamark pushes the meat to one side – "I'm not hungry" – and restful thought in the afternoon.

This Sunday afternoon, Croxford visits, unannounced.

"Are you," Mrs Seamark says, frowning, "staying all day?"

"Might be," he says, frowning back.

"Oh, not again," Claudia, their six-year-old daughter, sighs.

"What d'ya mean?" Croxford says.

"Nothing," she sniffs. She gets up, runs outside.

Sitting at the kitchen table, Seamark falls asleep. Mrs Seamark stands, collects the plates and cutlery, goes over to the sink. Seated, Croxford picks up the Bible, opens it, reads.

When Mrs Seamark has finished washing and drying, she turns towards Croxford.

Looking up, he smiles.

She turns back, looks out the window, watches her three children playing outside.

Toby and Jed are leaning against the shed door, stroking the dogs. Claudia is sitting on the ground, counting pebbles.

"If you give me a marble," ten-year-old Toby sniggers, "I'll show you the place where Daddy and Croxford killed the man and buried him near the cucumber patch."

Mrs Seamark opens the window. "Toby," she calls, "come in here now." She turns to Croxford. "Waken Tom this minute," she snaps.

Toby slinks in. Seamark is now awake.

"What," she says, " did you say to Jed?"

"If you give me a marble, I'll show you where Daddy and Croxford killed a man."

"What," Seamark says, "do you mean?"

"I watched you through the cracks in the floor," the boy says. "I saw you and him – " – pointing to Croxford – "and Uncle Ben and Uncle Richard kill Scottie and then chop him up and bury him in the garden and cook his hands and arms and legs and feet. His coat's in our chest upstairs and his walking stick's behind the – "

"Toby, you'll say no more about this to anyone,"

Seamark says, keeping calm. "Do you understand?"

Toby nods.

"Are you sure?"

Toby nods again.

"There's a good lad. Now go outside and play with your brother."

The boy runs out.

"What's he mean, Tom?" Mrs Seamark says.

"Nothing," he says. "The boy's always filled his head with make-believe and fantasy. You know that. But – " – standing up, scraping the chair on the floor, going over to her – " – if you mention this to anyone, I swear by everything that is holy, I will kill you without another thought and – "

Croxford stands next to them, his carpenter's wooden carving knife in one hand, the Bible in the other. "Swear on this good book," he snarls, the blade at her throat, "you will conceal all knowledge of this matter."

Her mouth drops open, her eyes alight, she shakes her head.

"Swear on this Bible," Croxford says, "or I'll slit your throat this very minute."

Northamptonshire
March-June 1764
5-8 months later

When carrying out his highway robberies, Tom Seamark doesn't keep to Northamptonshire. He goes as far as Market Harborough to the north – Leicestershire – and Rugby to the west – Warwickshire – bringing him jewellery, clothing, coins and banknotes – spending power without involving underhand traders or shifty middlemen.

He spends days, weeks, without going home, sleeping under hedges, in haystacks, abandoned barns, always caring for Buck, his Cleveland Bay. Buck's welfare is more important than his own. Without Buck, Seamark is lost and helpless.

Early March, having been a month on the road, Seamark and Buck are now outside Yelvertoft on their way home. A four-horse Royal Mail stagecoach trundles by. Passengers, mail, money, valuables. Easy, easy.

Not easy. Its driver and guard are old hands. The passengers always have their weapons ready. Worried by the shattering of gunshots, Buck rears, throwing Seamark to the ground. He's captured, tied up, arrested and taken to Northampton where he is convicted of highway robbery.

Monday, 23 April, 1764, Thomas Seamark, aged 33, is hanged on Northampton Heath until dead.

"John," Butlin calls out a few days later.

Croxford turns. He's walking along, smoking his pipe, taking the air in Guilsborough as a break from sewing coats all day. "Richard. You are well, I hope?"

"I hear some noise," Butlin says, "that you held a knife to Ann Seamark's throat and told her you would kill her if she spoke about – "

"Not true, my friend," Croxford says. "'Tis known, and always has been, that she is a lying bitch. I did nothing wrong."

Butlin, not satisfied, is afraid. He knows about Croxford's lack of restraint when faced by adversity and his ability to believe his own version of events which rarely match what actually happened.

He goes to his workshop – he's a glover and breeches maker – gathers together the little clothing he has, shuts his place and leaves early next morning. It takes him a long day to walk the thirty miles to Brackley where he knows he won't be known or recognised.

As the town is a coaching-stop on the Northampton-Oxford road with some thirty inns and pubs for travellers, Butlin doesn't stand out as a stranger. But the parish constable discovers him sleeping rough in a doorway, arrests him for vagrancy and locks him up.

It takes only a day to send a message to Northampton and receive a reply. Butlin is arrested again – this time for robbery – hauled back to Northampton, thrown in gaol to await the next Assizes.

"That's my coat," Gabriel Adams shouts, running across Hollowell Green. "That's my shirt."

A gentleman stops, turns.

Gabriel reaches him. "Sir, I pray, where did you

get the coat and shirt? They are mine. They were stolen from me some months ago. Who sold them to you?"

"Sir," the gentleman says, "I bought them from a workman in Guilsborough. Went by the name of Ben. Or Richard. I don't know. I swear he didn't know who he was. Few wits in his head, I'll wager."

"I thank you, sir. Will you be so kind to let me know your name and where the authorities will find you? I intend to find this thief and I will be grateful for your assistance."

Gabriel closes his smithy, tells Jessica, now his wife, he is going to Guilsborough. For the rest of the day, he patrols Guilsborough, asking after anyone called Ben or Richard. Someone mentions Ben Deacon. Someone else says he'll be found at John Croxford's workshop.

By the next morning, Gabriel has given a statement to the parish constable and the gentleman from Hollowell has been interviewed. Deacon and Croxford have been arrested for robbery, thrown in the County Gaol at Northampton – in the same cell as Butlin – to await the next Assizes.

After Thomas Seamark's arrest, trial and hanging, Ann, his wife, now lives in poverty. Three children to raise with only her income as a seamstress, she lives out of sight. Afraid of what could happen if the law notices them, she repeatedly warns Toby to keep his mouth shut, to tell nobody what he knows, to help his mother by being a good boy.

"You're the man of the house," she tells him.

Now eleven years old, Toby does as he's told. He helps around the home, he learns how to cook, he earns a few pennies doing errands for friendly neighbours.

He goes to school.

"Ha, Edmund Goosey," he shouts one morning break between lessons. "You're nothing but a stupid looby. Stupid goosey looby! Stupid goosey looby! Ya ya ya – "

Edmund runs at him. "Me, stupid? At least my dad's not a – " He kicks Toby in the shins. He's wearing clogs. He kicks Toby in the shins again.

"Aaah," Toby screams, hopping about. "You do that again – you do that again and I'll do to you what my dad did to Scottie – "

"Toby Seamark," a deep voice calls out. "Come here. Now."

"Yes, Mr Lyman," Toby says, hobbling across.

"Repeat and explain what you said to Edmund Goosey."

By the end of the morning, John Bateman, the local magistrate and employer of Jessica's first husband who died in a well trying to rescue a dog, and the parish constable are searching Catslo House, Ann Seamark's home. They find Scottie's walking cane in the pantry. They dig up a basket handle, ashes, piles of powder and bones, including a smashed skull, in the back garden. Ann tells Squire Bateman about

Croxford's knife attack on her.

In Northampton gaol, Croxford doesn't take long to give up Butlin and Deacon. All are arrested and charged with the murder of Thomas "Scottie" Corey.

Northamptonshire
Saturday, 4 August 1764
about 2 months later

After being found guilty and sentenced to death by hanging, Croxford, Deacon and Butlin are marched from Northampton Gaol to Northampton Heath, the place of execution. Soldiers from the 3rd Regiment of Dragoon Guards escort them all the way with fixed bayonets and muskets loaded with powder and ball.

After prayers with the minister, Croxford hands some papers to one of the gaolers and requests he read it to the crowd.

"John Croxford says," reads the gaoler, "'My character and behaviour were very good until January, 1760, when I got into bad company with Thomas Seamark. This proved my ruin. This much I confess. But I did not commit murder. I am not guilty of that crime.'

"Richard Butlin says, 'I have always been of good character. I am innocent of murder.'

"Benjamin Deacon says, 'I bore a tolerably good character until Christmas last, when I met Thomas Seamark. As a result, I committed various crimes. But I did not commit murder.'"

The gaoler says, "The manuscript goes on, 'We have been condemned on the false oath of Ann Seamark, the vilest wretch that ever appeared in a Court of Justice. There was not one word of truth in her evidence and that of her boy. It is a hellish and malicious contrivance of theirs to take away our lives.

"'I, John Croxford, was never with Richard Butlin until the Guilsborough Feast, which was about 25 October. I was near Catslo House with Richard Butlin and Benjamin Deacon only once and that was about 15 November. I was never in the house with them. They have testified that no murder was committed.

"'We have no doubt that the truth of this whole affair will be brought to light in time, although of little use to us today. We hope Ann Seamark will be properly rewarded and according to her just deserts. We will die in peace with her and with all the world. We bear no malice. We only hope that the great God will make known our innocence.'

The gaoler reads, "Written in Northampton Gaol the night before our executions. Let this be a caution to all good people. We, poor unhappy sufferers, have severally set our hands to this, it being nothing but Truth.

"The manuscript," the gaoler finishes, "is signed by John Croxford, Benjamin Deacon and Richard Butlin and dated Friday, 3 August, 1764."

After their executions, the bodies of Deacon and Butlin are hauled off to local surgeons for their use. Croxford's body is carried to Hollowell Heath in

Guilsborough where it is hanged in chains on a gibbet, erected especially for the purpose, where it is left to rot.

An Unknown Man

Tracy Smith

Alfred hurried along the road, the knuckles of his left hand white against the handle of his green leather briefcase. The fingers of his right were busy sweeping his thick, brown hair back from his forehead and checking his recently clipped moustache. Fastidious in his appearance, he'd formed the habit in his early twenties and repeated it many times a day.

His heart racing with exertion and nerves, he cried out in surprise when he heard a whoosh and a bang as a rocket exploded, sending coloured lights across the sky.

It was long after midnight. He thought the Guy Fawkes celebrations would have ended by now.

As he rounded the bend, he saw two figures turn in from the road to Northampton. They were coming his way. He threw himself against a hedge, cursing the cloudless, moonlit night, hoping he hadn't been seen. He had to find somewhere to hide. And quick.

The tall and impenetrable hedge ran along the road for some distance. It was impossible for him to get to the other side of it without being spotted and he couldn't go back the way he'd come.

Then he noticed that, a few feet ahead, the earth had cracked and sunk, sloping away to leave a ditch deep enough for him to hide in. He crept into it, grateful it hadn't rained for several days. He'd have hated to ruin his new spats and muddy his brown wool trousers.

He squatted, head down to make himself as small as possible. The smell of petrol and smoke lingered in his nostrils as he waited for the strangers' approach. It wasn't long before he heard their voices, young men laughing and singing, they sounded drunk. He'd wait until they'd passed and were out of sight before moving on.

But, as the voices grew closer, his mind became troubled.

What if they saw the fire and decided to investigate?

What if they realised it was a car and extinguished the flames?

What if they rescued the body while it was still identifiable – or worse – still alive?

He had to do something to put them off the scent before they even realised there was one.

He stood up.

The men, now only thirty or so feet away, stopped in their tracks, mouths open. The taller man grabbed his friend's shoulder.

Alfred stepped out of the ditch as if it were a perfectly reasonable place to have been and walked towards them with confidence and purpose. The men watched as he passed them on the other side of the road. He imagined they thought him a fine figure.

"It looks like a bonfire got out of control," he called out casually, sweeping his left arm back to where a red glow grew in the distance, to the spume of black smoke behind him. He hoped his words were enough to curb their curiosity. As he marched on, he congratulated himself on his quick thinking.

He stopped at the junction, took a white handkerchief from the breast pocket of his jacket and knelt to clean his spats. Then he stood up, brushed himself down and started walking towards Northampton, grateful now for the moonlight illuminating his path.

He'd been walking for only a few minutes when he heard the guttural coughs of an engine behind him. It was a delivery truck.

Alfred waved it down. "Are you going to London?"

"Yes" the driver said. "Open the door, Edwin. Are you getting up?"

Expressing his gratitude, Alfred climbed into the truck and settled into the cracked, leather seat, making sure his jacket didn't come into contact with the grimy youth beside him.

"What are you doing out here this time o' the morning?"

Alfred told him he'd arranged to get a lift from his friend who drove a Bentley and he hadn't turned up.

The men, suitably impressed, extolled the virtues of the Bentley and other motor cars in general and then, running out of things to say to a man of his obvious calibre, fell silent.

Grateful for the quiet, Alfred closed his eyes. Things had taken an unexpected turn. He wanted to be alone with his thoughts.

* * * * *

He'd picked up the hitchhiker on a whim.

He was usually very fussy about who he allowed to ride in his precious Morris Minor but he'd been driving for hours. The hiker was an opportunity to alleviate the boredom.

The man reeked of drink.

Alfred, disgusted by the man's unkempt appearance, wondered how anyone could go around like that. How glad he was to be successful, a respectable member of society. He was well-groomed, had good manners and drove a decent car. He wouldn't look out of place in any club, even one frequented by the finest of men. He enjoyed telling his passenger about his accomplishments, sometimes exaggerating them, as he was prone to do.

The man told him he had no family and no fixed abode. He worked as a travelling labourer and was making his way to London in the hope of finding work and lodgings to see him through the winter.

Alfred told the man how sorry he was that he was

all alone in the world and then told him about all the wonderful people he had in his own life: his wife, his children and especially his mistresses.

The man was awestruck.

Alfred, imagining how exciting his life must sound to someone who had so little, described in great detail how his work as a travelling salesman for the Garter and Braces company afforded him the opportunity to meet women from all across the country. He related how he'd wooed each one and how he juggled his many relationships and had even fathered children without a single one of them knowing about any of the others.

He led a charmed life.

He joked about the impact on his pocket. The financial strain of paying child maintenance orders and contributing to several households whilst keeping up appearances and running an expensive car.

He talked about it casually, belying the undercurrent of fear he harboured that eventually his debts would ruin him.

What he didn't say was how miserable it was at home. How he longed to be away from his wife. Those eyes once full of love and adoration now looked at him with distaste and accusation. He didn't tell the man that the thrill of his dalliances never lasted for long, that the shine of the new soon wore off to reveal the flaws he'd been trying to hide. How it was no sooner he'd declared that a love was for life than he was heading out the door to never look back.

He didn't admit those things to the man because he hadn't admitted them to himself.

He was shocked when the man, whom he judged beneath him in all things that counted in life, said, "That sounds like a nightmare. I couldn't live like that. I like a simple life. If it were me, I'd disappear."

The hairs stood up on the back of Alfred's neck. He drove on in silence, staring at the road ahead, seething. Who is he to judge me? He doesn't compare. What does he have to offer the world? Nothing. The sad wretch is no use to anyone. Dead or alive.

He distracted himself with thoughts of Ivy Muriel, how she adored him and how good they looked together and after a while the tension left his shoulders.

The man snored softly beside him.

Alfred thought about what he'd said. There might be something to it.

If he disappeared, so would his debts. So would his wife. He could start over with Ivy. Free of the chains that held him back, he could be an even better man. The man he was born to be.

Had fate thrown the stranger into his path?

Perhaps he wasn't so useless after all.

He left the main road at the next exit. The sign pointed to Hardingstone. It was quiet. There were no houses nearby and no other vehicles on the road.

Alfred parked the car and shook the man's shoulder.

"I'm going to fill her up."

He climbed out of the car, lifted the bonnet and unscrewed the petrol cap. Then he took a petrol can, his briefcase and a mallet out of the boot. He placed the can and the briefcase on the grass and the mallet inside his jacket.

"I'm going to have a smoke," he said. "Would you like one?"

Nodding eagerly, the man joined him at the side of the road. Alfred lit the man's cigarette and then his own.

"I need a piss," the man said and stumbled to a nearby tree.

Taking the mallet in both hands, Alfred swung at the back of the man's head as hard as he could. His knees buckled and Alfred, fit and muscular, caught and carried the thin man back to the car with ease. The man's throat gurgled as Alfred threw him face down across the front seats of the car.

He bent the man's legs so all of him was inside and hurriedly doused the body and the car seats with petrol. He flicked his lighter and held the flame to the hem of the man's trousers.

When the fire had taken hold, he slammed the car door, picked up his briefcase and fled.

* * * * *

He was roused from his thoughts by a hand on his sleeve.

"We've arrived," the spotty youth said.

Alfred thanked the men and walked the mile or so to his home.

In the perfect scenario, he would have packed a bag with the things he needed for his new life but he hadn't been able to plan ahead and had no choice but to return home one last time.

He let himself in and crept upstairs. Lily was still in bed and stirred when he went into the room.

"Alfred, is that you?"

"Yes, my dear. It's only me. Go back to sleep."

The dresser drawer squeaked as he pulled it open. He took out the pile of money he'd put aside for the rent.

"What are you doing?"

"Packing a bag. A few things I need for work."

"You're going to see her, I suppose," she grunted. "Your fancy woman."

He didn't reply.

He didn't have time for hysterics.

He stuffed a clean shirt and underpants into his attaché case and left.

He never wanted to see her again.

* * * * *

Big Ben chimed eight as he reached the Albert Embankment but the Elgin said it was two minutes to. His new wristwatch had come all the way from America and had cost him more than he could comfortably afford. He decided not to adjust it.

Brightly coloured charabancs were lined up by the side of the road and amid the comings and goings of the passengers, a familiar uniform caught Alfred's eye. A young man helping an elderly woman on to a coach wore a navy, blue jacket with two stripes on the sleeve. He was a porter for The Villier's Hotel nearby.

"Excuse me." Alfred approached. "I wonder if you could help me. I've had my car pinched and I need to get to Wales."

"Certainly, sir," the porter said. "There's a booking agent around the corner. I can take you there now."

Alfred followed the porter to a small dingy office with a large blue and white sign above the door: "Thomas Transport Co Ltd."

A bell rang as they stepped inside. The porter introduced him to the manager, Mr Farmer, then wished him well and left.

"I want to get to a place near Newport in Wales," Alfred told the short, smartly dressed man. Farmer shook his head.

"Unfortunately, our coaches don't go that far. But," he held up a finger and smiled. "We can find out who does... Robert," he called to a bald man sitting at a desk in the corner, "Our friend here needs to get to Newport, Wales. See what you can do."

The clerk nodded, picked up his telephone receiver and dialled. "It shouldn't take long, sir."

"Thank you, I appreciate it. I had my motor car stolen last night." He paused for effect. "A brand, new Wolseley Hornet." He enjoyed the hint of envy in the other man's eyes.

Farmer, the manager, whistled through his teeth. "Isn't that their latest model? I wouldn't mind one of those myself."

"Yes, that's right. I've only had her a fortnight. I stopped at a coffee stall and when I came out, she was gone."

The man shook his head in sympathy.

"To make matters worse, I lost my Stetson too," he said, pointing to his head. "It was on the front seat."

Farmer shook his head again, then shrugged his shoulders as if to say, "What can you do?"

"How long will it take to get to Wales?"

"Around eight hours, I would say."

"The Hornet could do it in three," Alfred sighed.

The clerk interrupted with a cough.

"Black and White have a seat available for you, sir. Their coaches are parked by the bridge. You can't miss 'em."

"Black and White, eh? I hope their coaches are as fun as their whisky," Alfred joked as he left the building.

The coach left the embankment at nine o'clock. Alfred sank into the only available seat with just a few minutes to spare. He was seated next to a portly gentleman with gold-rimmed spectacles and very little hair. The last remaining strands were hanging on for dear life and Alfred wondered why the man had let himself get so fat.

"A fine day for it," the man remarked as raindrops spattered against the window. "Would you like a sherbet lemon?" He held out a small, white paper bag.

"No, thank you," Alfred said. "It looks like I got on in the nick of time."

"Are you travelling for business?"

Alfred wasn't surprised that he would think so, looking as professional as he did.

"Not today. I'm returning to my wife in Cardiff. Unfortunately, my motor car was stolen last night."

The man tutted and sucked on his sweet. "I'm sorry to hear that. You can't trust anybody these days."

"You're right there. I'd stopped at a coffee stall in St Albans. I'd only left it for a few minutes."

The man tutted again, crunched his sweet, swallowed and then popped another into his mouth. He sucked on it for a time and then said, "I used to drive a motor car. An old Ford it was. I got rid of it, though. Much to the wife's relief."

"Really." Alfred was bored already.

"Yes," he chuckled. "I'm not a very good driver. I kept bumping into things. I had to hammer the dents out so many times I took to carrying a mallet in the back."

Alfred laughed and confessed that he too, carried a mallet and for the same reason.

"Those blasted wings dent so easily." The man bent forward and pulled a book out of his bag. A

Bible.

Alfred sneered. He promised himself that, if he ever read a book, he'd make sure it was a more entertaining one than that.

Suddenly dog-tired, he closed his eyes. He couldn't remember the last time he'd slept. However, whether it was the bumps in the road, the chatter of the other passengers or the unusual events of the night before, sleep would not come.

When the coach pulled into Cardiff Station, he said goodbye to the man, thanked the driver and dragged his weary feet to where the taxis waited.

* * * * *

It was half-past eight when Alfred walked up the front path to Primrose Villa, Gellygaer, Caerphilly. He was expected. His soon-to-be father-in-law, William Jenkins, had sent him a telegram a few days before, urging him to come quickly for Ivy Muriel had become seriously unwell.

He found William in the drawing-room.

"Oh, my dear boy, I'm so glad you're here." He pushed himself out of the chair.

"Oh, Dad. I've been a long time coming, about eighteen hours." He put his attaché case on the floor and shook the man's hand. "I had my car stolen at Northampton. I went in to have a cup of tea and when I came out my car was gone."

William patted Alfred's shoulder.

"My hat and bag were in the car. I've got her insured but I don't want that. I want my car."

"That's bad luck, son. I'm sorry for you, I really am but… Ivy."

"Oh, yes. Ivy. How is she? I've been so worried."

"There's been little improvement, I'm afraid." The old man wrung his veiny hands. "The doctor has confined her to bed and says she may have to stay there until the baby is born, perhaps longer."

"I'll go up and see her now."

Alfred tapped on the door and entered Ivy's bedroom. He was struck by how lovely she looked, even now with her pale face against the violet pillowcase and her unstyled hair. Yes, he would be proud to be seen with her on his arm.

"Alfred, is it really you?" she asked, her voice weak.

"Yes, my darling. I came as quickly as I could. I've been so worried about you."

He crossed the room and sat on the bed, taking her clammy hand in his.

"I must look a sight."

"Hush. You've never looked more beautiful."

Ivy smiled and was then overtaken by a fit of coughing. Spittle flew out of her mouth and Alfred turned his face away to hide his distaste.

"I've worn you out already," he said, standing up. "I'll leave you to rest. You need to keep your strength up."

"You're not going?" she pleaded, her eyes red and

watery.

"I'll only be downstairs. Try to get some sleep."

He moved towards the door.

"I'll dream about us and our future together," she smiled. "I can't wait until our house is ready. How much longer will it be?"

"Not long, my love. Not long."

His stomach clenched as he reached the bottom of the stairs.

William had made his famous pea and ham soup and it had never smelt better. Alfred sat at the dining room table and blew on his soup as William buttered two slabs of white bread and placed them on the small, willow-patterned plate next to his bowl.

"Thank you, Dad. I'm famished."

As William sat down, the front door opened and a voice called out.

"It's only me."

"Come in, Reakes. We're having our supper."

Mr Reakes, William's neighbour, stormed into the room, red in the face and waving a newspaper.

"I'm sorry to call so late," he blustered. "But I've just seen this in *The Daily Mail*…Oh, hello Alfred, I didn't see you there. But this concerns you. It's your car."

He threw the newspaper down on the table and prodded at it with a stubby finger.

Alfred picked it up and studied the photograph of the burned-out Morris Minor.

The accompanying article was short and said only

that a car had been found in flames by two men at two o'clock in the morning on the sixth of November in Hardingstone, Northamptonshire. The owner was not known and the police were investigating.

"That's not my car," he scoffed, throwing the newspaper back down on the table.

Reakes picked it up and stared intently at the page.

"But… I could have sworn."

"Alfred's car was stolen last night, wasn't it, Alfred?" William said. "Are you sure it's not yours?"

"I think I'd know my own car," he snapped. All he wanted was to finish his soup in peace. Why did everyone insist on bothering him so?

Mr Reakes, disappointed, bade them a good night and the two men ate their supper in silence. A couple of times, William cleared his throat as if to speak but he kept his thoughts to himself and Alfred was thankful for that.

Alfred pushed the empty bowl away, stretched and gave a long, loud yawn.

"If you don't mind, I'll hit the sack," he said.

"Of course. You look done in."

"Shall I sleep in the spare room, so as not to disturb Ivy?"

"I think that's best. Sleep well, son."

* * * * *

Alfred was marching down a long corridor, one man in front of him, two more behind. The sound of their boots echoed and bounced off the high, grey walls.

The lead man called a halt.

They stopped.

Then he stepped to one side and Alfred saw it.

A rope.

It hung perfectly still in the empty, white space before him.

His breath caught in his throat and he stepped back into the men behind him.

They closed in and, each grabbing one of his arms, led him to the noose.

"You have been found guilty," they chanted as a hood was placed over his head.

He felt the scratch of the rope against his throat.

* * * * *

Alfred woke with a start, his heart pounding and sweat running down his sides. He pushed the blankets back and sat up. He told himself it was only a dream but this was unlike any nightmare he'd ever had – this one could come true. He reassured himself that it had been a smart move to come to Wales, to have put so much distance between himself and the crime but he found little comfort in it.

He tossed and turned through the rest of the long night. When light came through the curtains, he heard William moving quietly around the house and then the soft closing of the front door as he left for his morning walk.

Alfred got up and went into the kitchen where he was surprised to see Ivy's sister, Phyllis, sitting at the table.

"Oh, good morning, Phyllis. I didn't know you were here."

"Good morning, Alfred."

She poured some tea into a cup, added milk and stirred. She pushed the cup across the table.

"There's a photograph of your car burned in the newspapers," she said, staring at him. He supposed she'd been gossiping with Reakes instead of minding her own blasted business.

"How do you know?"

"Your name is underneath the photograph." She held his gaze as if daring him to disagree.

Was she joking? He couldn't tell.

"Where is this newspaper? Show me."

Phyllis left the kitchen and Alfred reached for his tea but the cup rattled against the saucer and he couldn't steady his hand. He placed it back down spilling tea on the white tablecloth.

"There."

Phyllis came back into the room and handed him a copy of *The Herald*.

It was the same photograph of his car but this time the article said that the number plate, which had only been partially destroyed, had enabled the police to identify the owner as Mr Alfred Arthur Rouse. They asked that he, or anybody that knew him, contact the police as a matter of urgency.

The number plate.

Why hadn't he thought about that?

He rolled the paper up and put it in his back pocket.

"I didn't think it was mine. I'm going in the garden for a smoke."

He needed to get away from her stare and the questions that would inevitably come.

He lit a cigarette, gripping the lighter in both hands to steady the shake and, in case she was watching from the window, tried to appear relaxed.

They know who I am.

Visions of his new life faded away. It was a fantasy. It had always been nothing but a fantasy.

Why had he listened to that man? That fool? Disappearing hadn't made his life simpler. It had never been more complicated.

He cringed when he thought about how many people he'd spoken to over the last day or so. How many different stories he'd told.

If only he'd had more time to plan – or better still – hadn't picked up the hiker at all.

He wished he could turn back time. His life wasn't better now. It was worse, much worse. And to cap it all, he didn't even have a motor car. The shame of it.

He had no choice but to return to London. To report the theft.

To delay or to do anything else would look like guilt.

"Bit nippy this morning."

It was Brownhill walking his dog.

Alfred waved. Brownhill had a car.

"Mr Brownhill, can I ask you a huge favour?" he said. "I need to get back to London urgently and my car's been stolen. Can I trouble you for a lift into Cardiff?"

"Stolen, you say? Mmm…Yes. I can take you, I've nothing else planned for today. Let me finish walking Barker here. I'll be about half an hour. Does that suit you? Will you meet me at my house?"

"That's perfect. Thank you so much. I'll see you soon."

Alfred stepped back into the house and went straight to the spare room to collect his things. He paused at the foot of the stairs. He ought to go up and say goodbye to Ivy but what was the point? She'd find out he'd left soon enough.

He walked out of the house, glad to be leaving before William returned.

* * * * *

"I'm sorry to hear your car's been stolen," Mr Brownhill said. "A beautiful car that, so well kept, I'm not surprised she'd be a target for thieves. Have you reported it?" he said, gripping the steering wheel tight and peering through the windshield.

"I've reported it to the police and the insurance company."

"You have nothing to worry about if you've done

that."

Alfred thought that was a strange thing to say.

"What exactly happened?"

"Oh, it's too lengthy and complicated to go into." Alfred gave a dismissive wave of his hand.

Brownhill got the message and changed the subject.

After a few miles, he pulled into the gravel driveway of a large hotel. The Cooper's Arms.

"A friend of mine owns the place and I have some business to discuss with him. Come with me. It won't take long."

Alfred followed him in, where he was introduced to Mr Morris.

"This gentleman has lost his car and it has been found burned."

Morris shook his head and gave his condolences.

Alfred explained he'd gone into a restaurant in London for dinner. When he came out, he found his car was missing. He didn't know it had been burned until he saw it in *The Daily Mail*.

While he was talking, a butcher's boy came in with a box of sausages. After politely waiting for the men to finish their conversation, he said, "They found the charred remains of a lady in the car."

All three turned to Alfred.

He covered his face with his hands. "Oh, dear, oh dear. I can't bear to hear anything about it."

He left the hotel and waited for Mr Brownhill in the car.

* * * * *

He was dropped off at Melville Street, Cardiff, where he boarded an omnibus bound for Hammersmith. The top deck was virtually empty and Alfred sat at the back where he wouldn't be disturbed.

As he fingered his moustache, he remembered something.

Not long after picking up the hiker, he'd been flagged down by a police car. One of his taillights was out. He'd thanked the officer for letting him know and promised to replace the bulb first thing in the morning as soon as the garages were open.

He didn't know if the policeman had taken note of his number plate but it was probable. Even if he hadn't, photographs of his car had been all over the newspapers and he was sure to have recognised it.

Had the officer noticed there were two men in the car? He must have. He'd been trained to notice things.

He'd have to change his story. He had a sharp mind. It shouldn't be too difficult to come up with something. All he had to do was get the details straight.

* * * * *

He'd say he picked up the man on The Great North Road.

"He seemed a steady sort of chap, said he was

making his way to the Midlands. I must have got distracted by our conversation because I suddenly realised I was lost. Then the engine started spitting, so I turned off the main road to fill her up with petrol."

That would explain how he'd come to be on the Hardingstone Road.

"I'd taken the petrol can out of the boot and lifted the bonnet when I was immediately overcome with the need to relieve myself. I asked my passenger if he'd mind putting the petrol in while I went down the road for some privacy."

It sounded plausible.

But then he remembered he'd been carrying his briefcase. Had the men he'd encountered seen it? What if they mentioned it to the police?

"He seemed very curious about it and I'd caught him looking at it several times. I didn't trust him with the contents so I took it with me."

A reasonable stance. After all, who would trust a stranger with their valuables?

"I was fastening my trousers when I noticed flames behind me. I ran back as fast as I could. The car was on fire. I could see the poor man trapped inside. I tried to help him. I really did. But the flames kept beating me back."

Could a car burst into flames like that? Was it believable?

"I'd given him a cigarette but he said he wanted to save it for later. Perhaps he'd spilt petrol on his trousers. Perhaps he'd dropped a match. Oh, what a terrible, tragic accident."

And what of his behaviour after?

"I ran down the road to try to find help."

Why hadn't he asked the men for assistance? That was a tricky one.

"Guilt. I felt responsible for the man's plight. I was the one who'd asked him to fill the car. I gave him the cigarette. If it weren't for me, he'd still be alive."

He'd blame his lack of action on emotional turmoil and the chaos in his mind.

"I didn't know what to do. I panicked. In fact, I don't know much about what I've done since. I suppose it's due to shock."

That would go some way to explaining why he hadn't gone to the police and why he'd travelled all the way to Wales.

He spent the rest of the journey going over his story, refining the details, checking for contradictions.

* * * * *

The bus pulled into Hammersmith Bus Terminal at just gone half-past-eight.

Alfred stepped off the bus.

He saw a policeman standing under a lamppost.

The policeman looked at a piece of paper and walked towards him.

Alfred held his breath. This is it.

"Alfred Arthur Rouse?"

"Yes."

"I have some questions for you. I must ask you to accompany me to the station."

"Very well." Alfred dropped his shoulders as if in resignation. "I am glad it's all over. I was going to Scotland Yard about it. I am responsible. I am very glad it's over. I have had no sleep."

Afterword

Alfred Arthur Rouse was found guilty of murder at the Court of Northampton on the 31st of January, 1931.

He was hanged in Bedford Gaol on the 10th of March of the same year.

The body of Rouse's victim was buried in the grounds of St Edmund's Church in Hardingstone, Northamptonshire. His identity remains a mystery to this day.

His gravestone bears the inscription:

IN MEMORY OF AN UNKNOWN MAN
DIED NOV 6 1930

The Silver Hornet

Gemma Croucher

The roaring heyday of the Silver Hornet public house was well and truly over. By the mid-1980s, the people's choice of indulgence was no longer a pint but an illegal snowy white powder.

And so it was, during the decade of big hair and even bigger shoulder pads, the Silver Hornet fast became a big nuisance to the local people of Kings Heath.

It became a big nuisance to, in particular, the local police.

The Silver Hornet had had more temporary landlords than anyone cared to remember. The original landlord lost his licence for persistent after-hours drinking which, the police felt on reflection, was preferable to what was going on now.

Drug taking and drug pushing were commonplace. Known faces used the place all hours of the day and night. But no matter what intel the police had, how ahead they thought they were, they never caught anyone in possession.

But it went beyond that. The police were never

able to catch anyone with anything: drugs of any colour or class, dodgy home-made fivers or even highly profitable forged MOTs.

They *knew* what was going on as sure as they knew their own names. But there was no evidence.

Nothing.

Nada.

Zip.

It was a public embarrassment.

Located just beyond the junction between Mill Lane and Gladstone Road, the Silver Hornet's run-down appearance had also become an embarrassment to the local residents.

The top floor windows were haphazardly boarded up and the bottom ones filthy and neglected. The ornate Victorian building looked like a sightless dead body left to decay under the scrutiny of all who passed by. The place was at rock bottom. Most locals, at first concerned about the rise in crime, were now concerned that the dilapidated building would lower house prices. No-one would want to move anywhere near the Silver Hornet.

Criminals were in and out of the place all day long. Ordinary people gave the place a wide berth, put off by the duff-duff thud of blaring music and the acne-encrusted yobs lounging in open-topped cars. The police, who occasionally drove by, didn't need to tax their brains too hard to work out how these particular people afforded BMW convertibles when they never did a day's work.

Many of the older local men were saddened by the unsightly disrespect for the place. They remembered the good old days. Then, the Silver Hornet was a cordial centrepiece of this part of Northampton. They often recalled when, during the war, a bomb exploded nearby. It shook the old place so much that plaster fell from the ceiling into their beer. Not allowing Jerry to put them off, they carried on drinking their pints, plaster and all, as if nothing had happened.

On the opposite corner to the pub was a small, red-brick block of flats surrounded by its own grounds. In the corner property lived a couple of elderly pensioners, a world removed from the comings and goings opposite.

Mr Sam Fisher was, luckily for him, quite deaf. The consistent racket from the pub never caused him to miss a wink of sleep.

His wife, Violet, however, was not hard of hearing. She put the noise down to youthful exuberance.

Meanwhile their neighbours had reached the end of their patience. Several of them had complained to the police about the continuous noise, night after night. But it was the violent altercation that spilled out of the Silver Hornet one Friday night which escalated concerns.

Rumours spread around the local area about what happened around eleven-thirty that night. But, according to Dorothy Burt, a fellow resident in the little block of flats, these were the facts. Three men tumbled out of the pub doors in a moving heap of fists, elbows and knees followed by shouting, jeering spectators.

When Dorothy, a widow, complained to the police, she said the scene from her bedroom window reminded her of the bare-knuckle boxing match her father had taken her to see as a child. Rumour had it that the police found teeth on the street but Dorothy hadn't seen that and so it wasn't confirmed.

From the safety of her flat, Dorothy sat in the dark and watched the three men throw punches, push, shove and attempt head locks. Dorothy chose an unfortunate moment to blink for when she opened her eyes the fight had crossed over and moved into the flats' private grounds.

Suddenly the whole building shuddered. Then, a loud snap, a pause and an explosion of glass. Drunk, high and totally ignorant to their surroundings, the men went smack bang into the large lounge window of Dorothy's downstairs neighbour.

After such a public demonstration of lawlessness, the police had to act.

* * * * *

DS Mason and DC Barnes were assigned to stake out the Silver Hornet.

They had been rumbled once before, sitting in a van parked not so discreetly across from the pub. DS Mason still felt a flush break out on his face whenever the farce was mentioned. However, he optimistically accepted his role in the new investigation. This time, it would be different. This time, they were going to try to get co-operation from the public. Orders instructed them to go to the little flat on the opposite corner and get the resident's permission to use it for surveillance. This Sunday lunchtime. Sunday was the day when an awful lot of villains enjoyed a drink.

It was five-thirty on Saturday afternoon when Violet Fisher answered her front door to two smartly dressed men. Before she could say she wasn't interested in buying anything, the men covertly flashed their identification and asked to come inside. She allowed them in and showed them into the lounge.

The police officers were very impressed by the neat little room. It was as if they had stepped into a country cottage. A dark oak Welsh dresser stood against one wall with the most beautiful chinaware adorning it. Against another wall was a matching sideboard with perfectly polished silverware on display.

DS Mason was particularly impressed by the crisp whiteness of the many doilies and the lack of dust. Everything had been put together with an expert touch. Mrs Fisher was obviously an ideal homemaker. If it hadn't been for the large, modern windows, Mason and Barnes would've felt they were in another place altogether.

Sam Fisher was sitting in his armchair, reading. He looked up sharply.

"It's the police," said Violet, her voice unnaturally loud.

"Eh?"

"We're the police, sir," DS Mason said.

Sam gave a non-committal grunt.

Mason continued, "Of course, you'll both be aware of the events from a fortnight ago?"

Violet's gentle face hardened. "Yes. More than aware. Disgusting behaviour. Awful. Our poor neighbours. Broken window, glass all over the lounge floor." Shaking her head, she looked around at her own pristine living room. "Nearly gave both of them a heart attack being woken up like that. Lovely people too, our neighbours. Aren't they, Sam?"

"Eh?"

"Next door. Nice neighbours?"

"As neighbours go," Sam said, his eyes on his book.

DS Mason took the pause in conversation to go on and explain their request.

When he'd finished, Violet, quite flustered, watched her husband to see what he thought.

Realising the onus was on him, Sam shrugged his thin shoulders. "Please yourselves. I don't care." And with that, he picked up his book as if they were no longer there.

Still ruffled, Violet showed the men back into the little hall and agreed to let them in the following morning.

She went back in to her husband and half-shouted,

"Well, what do you think of that?"

But Sam had gone into yet another major sulk. "Don't know," he said, his eyes never leaving his book. "Don't bloody well care. I won't be here tomorrow. I'm going fishing. You deal with them."

Violet knew if she pressed him anymore, it would result in a row. She went into the kitchen and put the kettle on. She needed to think.

* * * * * *

Sunday morning was fine and clear. A perfect day for spying and fishing. In typical Sam fashion, he'd driven off in a huff, leaving Violet to do whatever she chose. She stuck to her usual Sunday morning routine and prepared a roast dinner.

At eleven sharp, before the doors of the Silver Hornet opened, DS Mason and DC Barnes arrived, their equipment concealed in a nondescript holdall. They decided the front-facing bedroom window gave them the best vantage point. Violet showed them up.

Mason and Barnes went about setting up their equipment in front of the large modern window which, as with the lounge, was out of place among the old-fashioned furniture.

Original fixtures from the tail end of the 1950s, although expensive at the time, now looked heavy and worn. The thinning orange and brown patterned carpet which, Mason guessed, was the newest addition to the room, clashed horribly with the lemon and pink bedspread. But he was impressed by Mrs Fisher's housekeeping. No dust could be seen anywhere. Ornaments and cosmetics had their own crisp white doilies. Even the two bedside tables had doilies waiting for the nightly glasses of water.

"What a nice woman," said Barnes.

"She certainly is. Shouldn't have to live opposite this godforsaken cesspit," Mason said, attaching the camera to the tripod.

"Too right. Old school, that one. Proper salt of the earth."

Mason sat on the end of the bed and looked through the camera, adjusting the focus. "This time, Barnes, this time, we'll get something. I've had enough of all the nonsense going on at that pub."

"Today's the day, Sarge," Barnes said. He really meant it. It was about time his DS got a break in this case. He clicked the binocular case closed and changed the subject. "Her husband seems a miserable old git, though."

"Never mind that now," said Mason giving him a side glance as he heard Violet approaching.

She opened the door while balancing a tray containing a cosy-covered teapot, two cups, saucers, teaspoons, a jug of milk, a sugar bowl with its own spoon and a packet of chocolate biscuits.

Barnes took the heavy tray from her. "That's magic. Thanks very much, Mrs Fisher."

"You won't need me for anything, will you?" she said.

"No, we'll be fine, Mrs Fisher," Mason smiled. "You just go about your day as normal."

An hour later, Mason and Barnes were perched on the end of Mr and Mrs Fisher's double bed, a camera tripod and an empty packet of chocolate biscuits between them. Mason looked at his watch again.

"It's half past bloody twelve."

Barnes had the teapot fully raised over his cup but nothing came out.

"Barnes, I said it's twelve-thirty."

"I heard you, Sarge. We've been here a whole hour. Waiting for something to happen."

"Something to happen? At this rate, we're waiting for someone, anyone, to just go into the bloody place. It's Sunday, for Christ's sake."

Mason picked up his binoculars.

"Sarge, we've got to consider the possibility there's been a tip off."

The debacle with the undercover van flashed through Mason's mind.

"No," he said, "it isn't possible."

* * * * * *

After Violet closed the front door on Mason and Barnes on Saturday evening, she sat and pondered the situation.

Sam's mood had escalated to the worst type of silent treatment. Not only would he not talk to her but he sighed or snorted at everything. She brought in dinner, quality sausages from the butchers, Sam's favourite, with creamy homemade mash and onion gravy. Sam sighed when she handed him the dinner tray, gave a wide smile and said, "They're your favourite ones."

But it was the snorting when she took out the dinner plates, when she brought in a cup of tea and, finally, when she turned on the television to watch *The Generation Game* that made her take drastic action.

"I'm going to take the chill off with a hot toddy," she said. "These May nights aren't warm. I'll make you one too, love."

Violet set her slate grey mortar and pestle on the worktop, dropped in four sleeping pills and expertly ground them up to a fine powder, which she tipped into Sam's drink. She added a dash more honey to take any bitterness away and gave the drink a final vigorous stir.

As she predicted, he waited a few minutes for it to cool, then drank it down in one.

Twenty minutes later, he was slouched in his armchair, snoring loudly, his book resting across his chest.

Now, she could enjoy watching the conveyor belt and see if anyone would win the cuddly toy.

More importantly, she could think in peace.

* * * * *

While the police achieved nothing in the bedroom

except eating empty calories, Violet divided her time between cooking the Sunday roast and looking out of her front room window at the pub.

After nearly two hours, she became increasingly agitated. Surely the police would leave soon? Almost as if her thoughts had made it happen, she heard the two men shuffling around and packing up. Straightening her floral pinny, Violet busied herself by checking her joint in the oven.

"Ah, Mrs Fisher, sorry to disturb you but we're heading off now."

Violet closed the oven door. "Oh, okay, Inspector."

"Thank you for accommodating us on a Sunday."

"No problem. I'm always home making the roast so it's no bother."

"And thank you again for the tea and biscuits," Barnes said, setting the tray on the worktop.

"Oh, you're welcome. Like I say, it's no bother. Let me see you to the door."

* * * * *

Violet watched them walk down her front path, turn right and cross over to wherever they'd parked their unmarked car.

Back in the lounge, she picked up the red telephone receiver.

"Gary? Yes, it's me. What the hell – "

"Are the coppers gone?"

"Of course they're gone," Violet snapped. "What do you take me for?" As she often did, she wondered how this idiot could actually be related to her. "Now listen to me, you gormless pillock, and listen good. You're already on thin ice with me over that fight the other week. If you can't keep people in line and I have to step in again, that means trouble."

"Sorry, Gran."

"You bloody well will be, Gary. How many times have I said I don't want any trouble? I'm doing all this just to top up my pension. Robbing government swine – "

The line was quiet for a moment while Violet composed herself. "Now, Gary, when I said call off today's job, what exactly do you think I meant?"

"Don't do the job. Like you said – don't go to the pub."

"And who did you tell?"

"Just a couple of fellas, Gran."

Quicker than she could say "Holloway Prison", Violet realised the message had reached all her local contacts.

"Gary," she said, "when I said call off the job, I meant call off operations. I said nothing about not going to the pub. I've had the police here all morning. In that time, not a soul has gone into the Silver Hornet. Not a single, bloody soul! You stupid idiot!"

In The Present

Moving On

Ashley Holthofer

We will shortly be arriving at – Northampton – please mind the gap between the train and the platform when stepping down from the train.

Sometimes I want to hide from the horrors of the world in the gap between the train and the platform. Part of me feels like the emotional horrors that haunt me wouldn't be able to find me there and I could exist as a folklore creature that terrifies young children – filthy, untormented and free.

I grab the handle of my hold-all from the luggage rack and haul it down. Packed to bursting because I never seem to be able to travel light. Most of what I own consists of useless trinkets and knackered cheap clothes. But I feel like they'd be lonely if I threw them away. Resisting the urge to slip into the gap, I step confidently from the carriage, over the vast 2cm gap and on to the platform at Northampton. It's an interesting day. It's the first day of my new life and I have a youthful, intoxicating sensation I haven't felt for many years.

My name is Jack Moreton and you find me picking

through the wreckage of my mind following the collapse of the most meaningful relationship of my life so far. I'm stalked by a sense of detachment and apathy that is familiar but unwelcome. I attempt to bat these harassing sentiments away as I present the screen of my phone to the QR scanner at the barriers, which dutifully swing open like the Gates of Troy.

I lock eyes with an officer of the Great British Transport Police as though she senses that I'm not from around here, or that something's off at the very least. I'm something that doesn't look right, doesn't feel right, doesn't think right. I live in a weird old world of my own, and there's nothing more comforting or more lonely. But I can never avoid the fact that my own world is encased within the world of the real, or reality, as it constantly insists upon being known. It's a grimy, nasty sort of place with dirty, jagged edges and large, cold corners shrouded in darkness, where the worst of the filth resides. The saving grace of this reality is the existence of beings who do not fear being cut by its edges or lost in its darkness, who gallop through it, attempting to shed a little more light on the place. One of these beings took me by the hand one day and told me to run with her. So I ran. But there's a weight inside me that I have always dragged along. The fatigue it invokes is potent and it's attracted to those darkened corners. It pulls me towards them like the slow, determined current of an icy river. And I lost her. She ran off into the distance and I was left in a jagged, dark corner that I did not recognise. This corner is called Northampton, and I'm here to stay.

As I stand on the station steps, it's a bright but blustery spring day. Scallies dart by on electric scooters along the pavement, weaving between the invariably downtrodden pedestrians. They do this with a degree of skill that I find unfathomable and part of me thinks that many of them must be secret geniuses held back by poverty and the temptation of a good time.

I descend the steps and hurry along, up the road towards the town centre.

I hit Gold Street. Gold Street hits me. This is more like it, I find myself thinking as I walk past people attempting to navigate clapped-out lives wrapped in sleeping bags and unshaven since 2020, fumbling for meaning in the most ironically named street in England. Why are they here? I don't know. Where did they come from? I don't know. I don't know a single – fucking – thing about them. I just know that they're down and out, done for the day and that it's a fucking disgrace. But can I honestly say that part of me doesn't share their despondency? That I can't see myself being in their shoes someday? I don't know. What would it take for me to give up? Sometimes I think I come pretty close, but I'll never be able to give you a definitive answer. I know that someday I'll be struck down for good and that I'll only be able to identify the cause in bitter retrospect.

Northampton is a nice town centre that's been

blighted by inconsiderate shopfronts, fast-food litter and bus stops that look as though they were designed by some kind of cretinous, vindictive android that sees the most profound beauty in the colour grey. Other aesthetic offenders are the scooters, painted bright – orange – because, heaven forbid, you didn't notice one that'd been dumped on the pavement (as they invariably are, in numbers that challenge the power of human reason), trip on it, fall into the road and have your head rolled flat by a double-decker bus that was designed by the same malevolent android that made the bus stop.

I arrive at my flat, situated close to the town centre. I collected the keys last week when I moved the majority of my things over from a city called Swansea, which resides not far from the edge of the known universe (or so it felt). It's a spacious flat that I'm renting – bright and airy which, coincidentally, is something that I've never quite managed to be. Can you tell? Maybe some of it will bleed into me as the months drag on.

Maybe I'll become happy-go-lucky, quit my job and buy a horse, move to the country and make my living as a window cleaner whose main trigger of dopamine release is the draw of his next breath. These kinds of people truly exist and I feel a deep, seething anger when I meet them as I know that, at a foundational level, I can never be like them. No matter how many times I'm told that I should be. The sun is out. And out I go to join it.

* * * * *

If I were told by some powerful, omnipresent being – who took the form of a mysterious cloud of twinkling hydrogen – that I must choose between either oxygen or coffee to go without for the rest of my life, I'd have to flip a coin. I hope this statement serves as a small window into the heart of my soul.

Speaking of, I find myself wandering up to what looks like a pleasant coffee shop. I step inside to the melody of a tiny bell and sit down by the window where I can watch the world go by. That intoxicating smell is in the air as a few grams of beans are electrically ground by the slim, fortyish man behind the counter, a tall forest of spiky silver hair nestled upon his head. I'm in my little piece of heaven upon this Earth.

I don't mean it, do I? Coffee or die? I'm the eldest of five and that gets to you after a while. Especially with a single mum and a distant dad. Without coffee, I really don't know if I could deal with that. I'm a shallow person and I do not make a single fucking apology for that.

The man behind the counter comes over to take my order and I begrudgingly realise that his personality is like the manifestation of sunshine indoors.

"Just a black Americano, please."

"Certainly, Brian," he smiles. "You're looking fantastic for your age, I must say!"

Maybe I should explain. In recent years, I have cultivated a natural hairstyle that, when I've recently blow–dried it, can be interpreted as identical to the hair style of Brian May from Queen. This may not have attracted so much attention in and of itself, were it not for the fact that, at the ripe old age of 28, my nose, jawline, eye colour and chin are uncannily similar to those of Dr May in his prime. As a result, I am often hailed as being said guitarist (despite not being able to carry a single tune on any instrument) whenever I walk into a public establishment. Part of me resents this fact, part of me couldn't live without it – and it's the latter sentiment that seems to win out. I'm a shallow person, and I do not make a single fucking apology for that.

I give the man a smile that is simultaneously both bashful and sickening and he goes off to make my drink.

The white walls of the small cafe are adorned with the most amazing hand-painted murals, some of which appear to draw their inspiration from quasi-Christian origins. There is one of a bearded man in some kind of robe drinking a cup of coffee in profile and another of a young mother, again in some kind of blueish, Biblical dress, clutching a baby wrapped in a brown blanket to her chest. She wears an expression of the most profound serenity on her face.

"Did you paint these?" I ask the man when he returns with my drink. It's just the two of us in the cafe at this particular moment.

His face lights up at the question. "I certainly did! Do you like them?"

I heartily admit that I do and I ask him where he learned to paint like that.

"I've always done it, I suppose. You know, a lot of people ask me that and I've never been quite able to describe how I know how to do it. I get the most wonderful images in my mind and I want to get them out into the world so people can see and experience them, too!"

I nod along to his answer, aware I'm coming under his spell and taking an interest. "Well, I'm certainly glad that you did." I find the images genuinely moving, they're wholesome and imperfect and lend the shop a character of its own.

"Do you mind if I sit down with you?" the man says.

I gesture for him to sit. Generally speaking, I prefer my own company. But I very much live by the philosophy that if something interesting comes your way, then you should embrace it no matter what. Just on the off chance.

"My real name's Jack, by the way." I mention as he takes a seat.

"I'm Bro – I mean, Martin, lovely to meet you!"

Brother Martin, as he will soon come to be known, is wearing a white, double-breasted chef's jacket. It has short sleeves through which his arm now protrudes to offer me his hand.

I shake it firmly. "Where did you get the

inspiration for your paintings?"

Martin doesn't flinch. He looks me square in the face as I take a sip of his nectar-like coffee. "God. In fact, it's He who gives me everything, not just inspiration."

I'm somewhat taken aback by this. It really isn't every day that you meet a card-carrying God-fearer.

"How does he speak to you?" It felt like the natural thing to ask, as strange as it sounds.

Martin smiles coyly at the ground. "In lots of ways. In dreams, in prayer, even in my everyday thoughts. He surrounds me. I don't think it's possible to escape His embrace. Do you hear Him?"

I take another sip of coffee and, momentarily, flash my eyes out of the wide window.

A parking warden slaps a yellow penalty notice on a car.

"I don't know what He sounds like," I answer. "I know inspiration and beauty. But I don't know where my own thoughts end and God's start with regard to these things."

Martin gives another coy smile at the tiled floor of the cafe. "He's everything, really. At least that's what I think. He's infused in your thoughts and permeates your consciousness totally."

"Were you always a barista?" I say, sensing that there's more to Martin than meets the eye.

"I was a monk for a long time. Brother Martin is often how I think of myself."

I smile in understanding. This is my first encounter

with an ex-monk, or any monk, for that matter. "And how did you end up in the coffee game?" I probe further, feeling Martin's excellent blend course through my veins. Another bashful smile.

"It was when we visited The Vatican, actually. Myself and the rest of my retreat went on a pilgrimage there. The Italian coffee was a revelation for me. I had to learn how to make it! While we were there I picked up as much knowledge as I could, made a few contacts and started practising when I arrived back home."

"So why aren't you a monk anymore?"

"The monastery where I was based was closed," Brother Martin shrugs, still smiling. "But I have a good life here. I spread The Word – as you're finding. God followed me, as He follows us everywhere."

I nod in admiration of his spirit. Quite vainly proud of myself for caring to probe deeper into a person and being rewarded for the effort with an interesting story. While I'm busy mentally patting myself on the back, Brother Martin breaks my train of thought.

"But there's something about you, something that I've seen before," he says, his bright eyes narrowing. "You're not quite right at the moment, are you? Heaven forgive me for saying – it's just that I've seen it before."

Brother Martin fixes his gaze on me as I look out of the window again, unenthusiastic about getting into the whole sorry affair.

"My partner split up with me not long ago." I reply, "I'm moving on."

Martin nods understandingly. "It's none of my business, really, but I can tell that something's not quite right. Would you like to tell me what happened?"

I take a moment to gather my thoughts. What did happen?

"I believe in each person's individual autonomy," I begin, "and that, in a relationship, you have no right to dictate how the other person should think and act."

"I think that's a very selfless approach to love," Brother Martin cuts in – if only he knew.

"But," I continue, "I've never before been with a person who, at the time, felt so right and yet in retrospect was clearly so wrong. We lied to ourselves and, in lying to ourselves, we lied to each other by extension."

"A relationship is nothing without honesty," Brother Martin adds understandingly, before I ask, "Do you think Satan resides within us all? As you believe God does?"

Brother Martin's expression falls a little at this, as though a feeling of dread has descended upon him. "I think fighting Him, and what He represents, is our eternal struggle. Do you think He was present in your relationship?"

"I'm not sure," I reply, setting my empty coffee

cup on its saucer. "I thought I knew her so well. I felt this closeness with her that had been totally alien to me until that relationship, an understanding and dependence that transcended everything I'd known previously. It felt as though there was this personality which represented the light of my reality, in which lay this appreciation for and forgiveness of the bare facts of my life and all the transgressions therein. I felt a peace that had been denied me all my life until I arrived at those precious moments.

"But it was wrong. It was false. It was all based on the false portraits of each other we had painted for ourselves and idolised. I don't know if I could trust myself again or whether I'll ever be able to tell the difference between a lover and my portrait of them until it's all too late. Do you think Satan lives somewhere within all that? I can't tell."

During my explanation, Brother Martin's face had settled into a plaintive expression that gazed off into a distant, shaded corner of the shop. A swift–moving cloud, driven by the day's powerful wind, suddenly obscures the sun outside, and the entire cafe is cast in its shadow. Brother Martin doesn't move an inch.

I glance at the murals on the walls, their bright colours now faded in the absence of direct sunlight. My fingers curl around the edge of the table, as the painting of the bearded man in profile locks eyes with me, still drinking deeply from his cup. I blink and turn towards the dark-haired mother holding the baby. Now, she's staring back at me with bright, hazel eyes, where, before, her eyes had been lowered to the baby and their colour hidden.

My heart rate accelerates at what I assume are hallucinations. The woman's image turns to face me square-on, the folds of her blue robe rippling as she does so. I feel a lightness in my chest as I look at her, similar to the feeling of waking with a lover knowing that a bright, empty day lies before you both. It's like coming up for air, being cured, flying.

The bearded man continues to stare at me knowingly out of the corner of his eye, as he sips his coffee. I look back to the woman, and the brown bundle that contains her child evaporates before me like the thick, grey steam rising from the bearded man's cup. Her arms fall to her sides and her dark eyebrows sharpen. At the corners, they begin to arc towards her temples and, at the centre, stretch down to the bridge of her nose. As the brow becomes heavy, her serenity is lost. Her smile extends unnaturally towards her ears and she lowers her head, so that she's looking up at me through her brow.

I'm not breathing now, and the bearded man continues to direct his knowing, sideways stare at me. The shop continues to fade into gloom and the woman's eyes darken until they are ink black. There's a whistling in my ears like wind rushing between the masts of a ship. It grows louder and louder while the woman's face becomes more grotesque by the second.

I stand suddenly to the clatter of my mug and

saucer, grab my jacket and rush past Brother Martin towards the door. But, as I pass him, he grabs me by the forearm and looks up at me with a panic in his eyes.

"You knew her emptiness better than your own," he uttered rapidly. "You need to give yourself the same love God gives you."

"It was lovely to meet you, Martin," I splutter before stepping out into the harassing wind and blinding sunshine.

* * * * *

Is he right? I ponder with hunched shoulders as I make my way briskly along the street. I run a hand across my face and blink hard, glancing back over my shoulder periodically.

Isobel – the woman in question – certainly agreed with Brother Martin's proclamation:

You don't love yourself, and you can't get around that fact by using me as a substitute.

Those were her words that Friday as the cold morning light seeped in through the window of her flat. My world cracked and through the crack escaped some essence of my life that has been lost to me ever since.

Do I hate myself? Hate. My word, not theirs. Is not loving yourself the same as self–loathing? If I do suffer from chronic self–hatred, it's a fault that resides so deep in my foundation that I genuinely can't identify it as something abnormal. It's simply how I think and how I am. How do I go about changing something like that?

These are my thoughts as I storm through the town, heading nowhere in particular, walking for the pure sake of it as the movement and rhythm help me process my thoughts. I'm always moving and shaking away from trauma and towards something that is fundamentally reassuring but impossible to define.

There's a pounding in my head as I find myself by the canal, under the gaze of the Carlsberg brewery looming large further down the towpath. The honking of Canadian geese pervades the afternoon, mixing humorously with the sound of The Cranberries leaking from the window of one of the riverboats moored nearby.

I take a seat on a bench and sit forward with my elbows on my thighs. The wind whips up the water, sending heavy ripples along the canal that shimmer in the bare sunlight. I stare into it. As the wind bellows along, my vision is soon blinded by the light reflecting off a particularly large crest of water. It strikes me like a spotlight. Then I am taken from this place. Into the space that resides somewhere between consciousness and dreams.

* * * * *

In this space, too, the wind bellows.

Along the Rheinland valley where it rustles the

autumnal leaves of vast forests and whistles through the ramparts of fairytale castles. A heavy layer of grey cloud smothers the valley, hugging the peaks of the hills visible over the river and shrouding them in uncertain gloom.

It's a place somewhere adjacent to my memory. On my European travels with Isobel.

Our train has broken down. Isobel and I stand on the edge of the track, the smoke from our cigarettes dissipating immediately in the wind. She is a short young woman with blonde hair dyed black, bright hazel eyes that unwillingly admit a deep sense of mischief and ears that protrude forward like those of a mouse. This strange woman forges one of the cornerstones of my reality. The depth of the connection that binds me to her invokes genuine fear within me.

"Why do you love me?" she asks with a teasing smile. Nicotine has always brought out her introspection, which often wantonly manifests itself when I'm in her presence. Accustomed to this kind of abrupt questioning, I smile and take another drag of my cigarette.

"I could tell you many flattering things," I say. "The things that I admire about you: the shape of your eyes, the glee of your smile, the smoothness of the soles of your feet or your sexual honesty. But the fact of the matter is that it can't be any one thing. You're more than the sum of your parts and I love the finished article. I just do. There's no explanation I can offer that will satisfy you, one which won't make my reasoning sound trivial in some way."

"Loser," she scoffs.

I shrug this off, grin and take another drag.

"Don't you want to know why I love you?" Isobel continues.

"It's enough for me to know that you do," I smile. "I'm not cruel enough to make you explain yourself to me."

She gives me a shove and I chuckle as I stumble a few paces. Isobel pouts her lips, I grab her from behind and plant a kiss on her tender cheek.

"Point proven," I note.

Isobel flicks the stub of her cigarette away.

"I do love you, Jack," she declares as she looks up at me. "In the mornings, when you're behind me and my whole back fits within the breadth of your shoulders. You're my whole world then. You're my whole, soft world," she smiles.

I kiss her again. She places her cheek against my chest. Then her eyes narrow and she points down the track. "Here comes another one now!"

She swiftly reaches into the pocket of her black greatcoat and produces a Polaroid camera which she hands to me. "Quick, quick!"

I turn the camera on and hug her shoulders with my free arm. We're right beside the track as the train approaches, hurtling along at cruising S–Bahn speed. I hold the camera up in front of us.

"All right, all right – here it comes! Three...

Two… One – "

I press the button. A blinding flash, the light of which captures the ecstatic expressions of a young couple as a speeding train rushes by meters behind them, sharing an electrifying energy as rare and precious as it is beautiful.

* * * * *

I'm back on the canal. The music from the riverboat has switched to something by The Cure.

I inhale deeply upon being repatriated to reality and steady my gaze on the water again. The fragility of my emotional stability becomes glaringly apparent in these moments. I have barely enough understanding of myself to pose questions, making answers impossible to imagine.

The wind blusters in my ears and I see those mischievous eyes before me again in the bright days of the past – but these images are suddenly cast in shadow and, somewhere within the haze of my memory, I catch the sideways glance of the bearded man, knowing and silent.

I stand up, walk towards the edge of the canal where I catch my reflection in the murky water. Like the woman on the cafe wall, my image is altered and distorted as the water ripples and swirls below me. My mind does the same. Ripples and swirls.

Family

Jo Purdon

Watford Locks might have been a picture-perfect location, but it was marred by the constant roar of the M1.

Adam tied Aurelia to a bollard, pleased to see there were no other boats waiting. He was about to book in with the lock keeper when he heard Richard, his father, shouting.

Richard pocketed his phone and perched on the stern rail as if he couldn't trust his legs to hold him. "You won't believe this," he said. "Philippa and I have been accused of trying to commit mortgage fraud."

"You and Flip would never do a thing like that," Adam scoffed.

"They're saying I inflated her income on the wage slips she submitted," Richard said. "I gave her overtime on the run-up to her application, that's all. These people put two and two together and come up with five. Your mum's picking me up from the services so I can sort this out. I'm sorry to cut our trip short."

"Don't worry, Dad. It's not like I haven't seen Crick before. I'll bring Aurelia home."

Secretly relieved, Adam wiped the sweat from his brow and cast off. He reversed a short way back, switched to forward gear to ease the bow into the notch of the winding hole and pulled the tiller hard over. The sixty-footer swivelled smoothly until she was pointing in the opposite direction.

A few minutes later, Adam moored the narrowboat while Richard locked the cabin. They climbed some steps beside a bridge, went a short way along Station Road and walked down a service road with a No Entry sign. After edging around a yellow barrier, they were in the lorry park of Watford Gap services. Heat haze shimmered over the tarmac.

It was a lengthy trudge to the building, which provided a welcome respite from the heat, but the hordes of people and bright lighting were a shock after the tranquillity of the Grand Union. Adam quickly adjusted. The buzz of the place was like an airport, people from all walks of life converging briefly on their way to God knows where. He felt like an interloper, having come from the waterway and knew most of these folk wouldn't even be aware the canal was there.

Richard answered his mobile, "Thank you, darling. I'm on my way."

Outside, Adam's mother, Xanthe, stood waving beside her sleek Porsche Boxster. She reminded him of a fifties film icon in a chic head scarf and sunnies.

He kissed her dutifully on the cheek and wished his father good luck.

Adam went back in and browsed in W H Smith's, picking things up and putting them down. He left without buying anything, having made a bold decision, and called the most recent contact on his mobile.

"Hey, babe." Kai's voice was husky like he'd just woken up.

"Not disturbing you, am I?"

A scenario popped unwanted into Adam's mind – that Kai had just woken up in someone else's bed following afternoon sex.

"No way," Kai said. "Saving me from sunburn, more like. I fell asleep on the sun lounger. How's it going?"

Adam pictured Kai in the garden on Wellingborough's Hemmingwell Estate and smiled. The pair had met on a night out in Leicester where Adam went to uni. They had been virtually inseparable since.

The first time Kai had invited him to his family home, he'd got lost and been approached by a group of trackie-wearing youths. They'd teased him about his posh accent, admired his whip – he was driving his mum's car – and demanded to know who he was there to see. When he mentioned Kai, their tone changed. It seemed Kai was well-liked. His mother, Deana, made Adam welcome and, in the three months he'd been seeing Kai, she had come to treat him like one of her own.

"Dad had to leave," Adam continued. "That's why I'm calling. I know it's your weekend off and I wondered if you fancied joining me on the boat?" He held his breath and listened to the silence. "You there?"

"Sounds sick," Kai said. "Only I've never been on a boat, apart from the rowing boats at Wicksteed Park. I dunno what use I'll be."

"You'll be keeping me company. I miss you."

"I miss you, too. Where you at?"

"Watford Gap services, northbound, near McDonalds. Bring overnight things."

"Cool. See you soon."

Adam bought a chocolate milkshake and settled down to people-watch. He was studying acting and believed the art was best learned by observing people going about their day-to-day lives. He sucked on his straw and watched people scrolling through their phones. It was like they needed to let the world know they were alone but not lonely. He watched couples interacting and tried to work out which one was in control. Up until now he'd been the follower in his relationship with Kai. Never once had he invited Kai to do something or go somewhere and was quietly pleased he had done so.

A mother with a crying baby took a seat at the next table. The infant quieted when the mum took her out of the car seat and cuddled her. At that point, Adam realised she was breastfeeding, so focussed his attention elsewhere.

Half an hour later, Kai appeared. He was wearing a small backpack over a pink and blue tie-dye T-shirt. They did an awkward half-hug.

"Would you like something to eat or drink?"

"I wouldn't mind a cheeseburger," Kai said. "I was gassed about seeing you and forgot to eat."

Adam grinned, pleased he had that effect on Kai. "You look after the table. I'll get the food."

* * * * *

Caitlin feared she'd used overkill trying to make Wayne understand how beneficial socialisation was for babies but, for once, his mum had backed her up. He'd finally relented and agreed to let her take Ella to Parents and Tots – as long as she sent him a photo.

He even let her use the car. One of the ancient Peugeot 306's cooling fans had stopped working, but Wayne was unemployed and claimed he couldn't afford to get it fixed. The car ran fine for short hops providing the heater was kept on full blast to take the heat away from the engine.

Caitlin drove past the venue in Dunchurch and joined the motorway heading out of Rugby towards Northamptonshire. At the point where the M45 merged with the M1 she noticed the car interior had become very hot despite both front windows being open. A smell vaguely like curry started coming from the vents. She almost laughed when her stomach growled. She hadn't eaten since the day before, having been too nervous to attempt breakfast. The temperature gauge was creeping steadily towards the red zone.

"Shit, shit, shit!" Caitlin said. "What are we gonna do, Ella?"

The oblivious baby gurgled and sucked her fist.

The sign for Watford Gap services appeared and, with a sigh of relief, Caitlin pulled in. She found a space, switched off the engine and opened the doors to let the smell out. She listened to the ticking noises coming from under the bonnet and sent a silent prayer of thanks that the car had got her this far.

Caitlin's phone alerted her to a message. Her hands shook as she opened it. Wayne. *Where's my photo?* Of course, she should have been at Mums and Tots by now.

She almost threw the phone when it started to ring. It was Wayne, naturally. She didn't quite dare to reject the call. Instead she let it go to the answerphone. He would be wanting to know why she hadn't sent the photo.

Another message. *Where are you?* Then another. *Come home now.*

She took deep breaths to steady her nerves, reminding herself she had somewhere safe to go even if she didn't have the means to get there. She called Nikki, her best friend from school and her saviour. Not only had she persuaded Caitlin to leave, but she'd also promised her and Ella a safe home.

"Hi, Caitlin. I'm at work right n– "

"Where?"

"Edinburgh. The big wedding I told you about, remember?"

Nikki worked as an events manager which meant she spent a lot of time away from her home on Wellingborough's Gleneagles estate.

"I've done it," Caitlin said. "I've left him. Only the car's overheated and I'm stuck at Watford Gap."

"Leave it and call a taxi. You know where the spare key is and there's cash in my bedside drawer if you need it."

Close to tears, Caitlin thanked Nikki and ended the call. She blew out a breath and tried to gather the strength to make her next move.

Another WhatsApp message. A screenshot of a pin on a map showing her exact location. *Last seen today at 13.13.*

Caitlin gasped. He knew where she was. But how? A tracker! He must have planted some sort of tracker.

She released Ella's car seat and frantically began searching the car. She felt down the back of the seats and under the dashboard but found nothing. She picked up the mats and shone her phone torch under the pedals and seats. What did a tracking device even look like?

It was now 1.19. If Wayne borrowed his mum's car he could be here in a matter of minutes. She thought about calling the police but, unless she could prove he'd committed a crime, she knew there was little they could do. Distancing herself from the car was the best plan.

She slung Ella's nappy bag over her shoulder and grabbed the handle of her car seat. She was about to run into the services and hide in the Ladies but spotted the footbridge and headed towards that instead. Wayne would find the car and assume she was here somewhere. He'd never think to look for her on the northbound side.

She made it into the food court just as Ella began to squall. Fear had suppressed Caitlin's appetite but she queued at the McDonalds' counter knowing she needed to fuel her body. The server sent her to sit down – she'd bring her food over. Caitlin collapsed into a chair and took Ella from her car seat. Well practised in the art of discreet breastfeeding, she brought the baby close before partially lifting her top.

Although she'd been taken into care at a young age and therefore had no firsthand experience of being mothered, Caitlin was determined to be a good mum and had read every book on pregnancy, birth and childcare she could lay her hands on. Getting away from Wayne was more important than ever with Ella to think about. It was also dangerous. He'd threatened to tell lies to Social Services to make her look like an unfit mother if she tried to leave. She needed legal advice urgently.

Surrendering to fatigue and the baby's rhythmic pull as she suckled, Caitlin zoned out and jumped when her Big Mac and Coke were placed in front of her. She chewed and swallowed her food without tasting it.

All Caitlin had ever wanted was a family of her own. She'd met Wayne eighteen months ago on a dating app. He'd promised her the world, but they'd ended up living at his mother's cluttered house in a Warwickshire village. It was only fifty minutes away from Wellingborough and everyone she knew but she felt so isolated it might as well have been the other side of the world.

The abuse was insidious at first. The constant texting whenever she wasn't with him under the guise that he worried about her. Then she had to send photos. She became familiar with the carpets and floor coverings everywhere Wayne took her because they were all she saw. If she looked up at anyone, he accused her of carrying on with them or wanting to. In the end, it was easier to stay at home.

The abuse escalated, became physical. It was always the same. Wayne would hit her. He'd apologise. Beg for forgiveness. All would be well for a few weeks. He'd slip. He'd do it again. Then the final straw. Still recovering from childbirth, she hadn't wanted sex, and he'd forced himself on her. He ridiculed her when she called it rape.

* * * * *

Adam threw their rubbish in the bin. Kai picked up his backpack, ready to go.

"That's fingertip bruising," Kai whispered. "I hope

she's leaving the bastard."

"Hmm?" Adam followed Kai's gaze to the mother of the baby at the next table and saw the marks on her upper arms. It looked like someone had gripped her very hard. "I suppose your mum's work makes you more tuned in to that sort of thing?"

"Hell, yeah." Kai unzipped his backpack and found one of the leaflets Deana had given him for occasions like this. "Excuse me."

The woman started, then looked at him.

"Let me give you this." He placed the leaflet on her table. "My mum works with Women's Aid. They can help you if you need it. Just bin it, if not."

"Thank you." Her eyes filled but she managed a smile. As she looked at her phone, it turned to a frown. She yelped and dropped it as if it had burned her.

Picking it up, Kai tried to hand it to her.

Gibbering, she put the baby in the car seat and upended the nappy bag, sending the contents all over the floor. Then she fell to her knees and scrabbled through everything.

"Are you all right?" Kai asked, even though it was obvious she wasn't.

"He's found us." She snatched the phone back and held up a screenshot of her current location. *Last seen at 13.54.*

"There's a tracker hidden somewhere," she gasped. "I – I thought it was in the car." She was heaving breaths, fighting not to cry.

Kai helped her to a seat while Adam gathered up baby things and put them in the bag.

"I'm going to try something," Adam said. "Bear with me." He opened an app on his iPhone and ran it over the nappy bag. A high-pitched jangle came from the table.

"It's found an AirTag. It's on either the baby or the car seat."

Caitlin scooped the baby up. "It can't be on Ella, I dressed her."

Adam peeled the cover of the car seat back. A small device with a silver Apple logo was Sellotaped to the moulded plastic. "Here it is. I'll take the battery out so he can't track you any further."

"He knows where I am *now*. He could be here any second." Caitlin's eyes were wide with fear.

"Don't worry," Adam said. "We'll walk you to your car."

Caitlin shook her head. "It's overheated. It won't get me to Wellingborough."

"I live in Wellingborough," Kai said. "You can take mine." He shrugged on his backpack and picked up Caitlin's bag. "Come on. Let's go."

He and Adam strode towards the exit, Caitlin hurrying after them.

"How will you get home?" Caitlin said as they approached a red Suzuki Swift.

"Adam's taking me on a boat trip," Kai said. "He won't mind running me home afterwards. See that sign? I've gotta pay twenty-one quid to leave my car here overnight. Sheesh! You'll be doing me a favour, hun."

While he unlocked the door and secured Ella's car seat, Adam gave Caitlin the disabled AirTag.

Kai exchanged numbers with Caitlin and handed her his car key. "Safe home. Make sure you keep that AirTag and report him. It's a crime to track someone without their consent."

The two young men watched her drive away, then looked at each other.

"I can't believe you just did that," Adam said. "Has anyone ever told you you're a beautiful person inside and out?"

"My mum might've said something like that, but she's kinda biased," Kai grinned.

* * * * *

"It's really peaceful here," Kai said when they got to the canal. "Who'd have thought Watford Gap was so close? I've always wondered why it was called that. I mean we're miles away from Watford and what's the gap all about?"

"Watford is a village just along that road we crossed. And the gap is a strip of low-lying land between the hills. The A5 comes through it – the old Watling Street – built by the Romans. Then you've got the M1, the canal and the West Coast Mainline. I don't sound like a show-off, do I?"

"Just a bit." Kai laughed. "This is called a transport

corridor. I remember that from school."

"That's right," Adam said. "And this is Aurelia."

Kai was like an excited kid as he looked around. "This boat's sick! It's got a proper kitchen and everything."

"On a boat, it's called a galley. The living area is called the saloon." Adam stopped himself in case he sounded like he was showing off again.

They got under way.

Kai stood with Adam at the stern where the throb of the engine drowned out the motorway. As they passed the lorry park, the bright trailers were clearly visible through the trees behind a strong metal fence.

Kai ducked needlessly as they went under an ornate old viaduct, which made Adam laugh, but suddenly the engine was straining.

"What's going on?" Kai said.

"Something's fouled the prop." Adam threw her into reverse in hope of shaking whatever it was off but the engine stalled. "It's nothing to worry about, but I need to move her out from under here in case another boat comes along."

He used the barge pole to push the boat out from the confined space, then hauled her to a safe spot along the towpath and secured the mooring lines.

"This is the weed hatch," Adam said as he opened the cover. "But I think they should re-name it the carrier bag hatch. Shouldn't take long." He put his hand in the water and pulled a face. "This is no carrier bag. Whatever it is, it's huge. Can you get the knife out of that locker?"

After much underwater slashing, Adam pulled out a foot-long piece of polyester wadding.

Kai looked closely. "That's part of a duvet, innit?"

"I believe so. The rest of it's still under there."

"Hope it's not king-size. Want me to have a go?" Kai said.

"No, I'll do it. The propeller's very sharp."

"Ha. Like I don't work with knives every day." Kai rolled his eyes. "I've got a message from Caitlin. They've got there safely and, bless her, she's put a tenner's worth of petrol in my car."

"Great news," Adam said, pulling out another strip of wadding.

"I'll make a cuppa, shall I?" Kai felt a need to do something useful, however small.

Over the next two hours, Adam managed to clear the prop but didn't dare start the engine with the bulk of the duvet still caught up under the boat. He looked up at the sky because it had gone prematurely dark. There was a rumble of thunder, then hailstones the size of marbles were pinging off the boat. He replaced the weed hatch and took shelter inside.

Eventually the hailstorm gave way to heavy rain.

Adam checked the weather on his phone. "It's supposed to rain half the night, apparently. I'll have to sort it in the morning. I'm sorry, this isn't exactly the peaceful mooring spot I had in mind."

Another rumble turned out to be a heavy goods train rattling and clanking its way along the track. The tremor vibrated up the mooring ropes.

"It'll be fun trying to sleep tonight," Kai said. "Maybe we could make earplugs. Got any cotton wool?"

"Nope," Adam said shortly, annoyed that someone had chucked a duvet in the canal in the first place and gutted they'd have to spend the night in such a noisy area.

"Toilet roll stuffed in the ears works," Kai said. "Two of my old boyfriends snored something chronic."

"Hmph." Being reminded about his lover's body count – one of Kai's phrases – made Adam feel insecure because Kai was his first and only. He switched on the interior lights and stomped towards each of the windows, yanking the curtains closed against the gloom.

Kai ignored Adam's moodiness. "What are we gonna do about dinner?"

There's not a lot in," Adam said. "Dad and I were going to have something at Crick."

Kai found a box of eggs. "D'you fancy an omelette, babe? There'd better be a whisk."

"Sounds good." Adam yielded, producing a balloon whisk from the drawer but didn't hand it over straight away because he wanted to make sure he had Kai's full attention. "*Do not* under any circumstances call me babe in front of my parents. And no physical contact. We're just friends as far as they're concerned."

"It's ridiculous," Kai scoffed, "to think you're twenty-one and haven't come out to your parents."

"I'm scared of disappointing them. I feel like I've already let Dad down by studying acting rather than something more conducive to running the business, like engineering."

"Your sister's got that covered, hasn't she?" Kai said.

"True. Flip knows everything from setting the machines to toolmaking and she loves it. Even if I make it as an actor, I'll probably end up there whenever I'm not in work anyway." He rummaged in the cupboard and found a tin of beans and the end of a loaf.

"What about your mum?" Kai said. "D'you think she'd be cool with it?"

"I don't know. Mum's hard to read. I got my love of acting from her, you know? She tried it when she was young but never got her big break. She does am-dram, but I don't suppose it compares to being a pro."

Adam left Kai to get on with the thing he did best – cooking. He was a commis chef in a pub near Wellingborough but was itching to climb the ranks.

Twenty minutes later, Kai called Adam to the little dinette table to eat.

"How do you make simple food taste like a gourmet meal?" Adam said. "That's the fluffiest omelette ever and the beans are literally bursting in my mouth."

Kai smiled. "It's a soufflé omelette. You whip up the egg whites, then mix in the yolks and season well. As for the beans, I added butter and overcooked them. That way they soften up and the sauce gets richer."

"You're amazing," Adam said.

Kai did something even more amazing by producing a box of home-made chocolate truffles from his backpack to round off their meal.

They slept in the double bed his dad had used, but Adam kept waking up. He couldn't shake off the worry that Kai might do or say something in front of his parents and give them away. He'd also been thinking about how to deal with the dastardly duvet under the boat.

Once it was light, he left Kai sleeping and stepped off the boat. A summer mist hung over the wet grass. Adam filled his lungs with fresh, clean air, enjoying the peace and solitude of early morning on the cut.

He loosened the stern line to give himself room to manoeuvre and used the boat hook to poke around under the boat. The hook burst through the rotting outer cover of the duvet. He twisted it to gather the polyester wadding, reminding him of candy floss. When he pulled on the pole, the duvet came out from under the boat, billowing in the water like a monstrous jellyfish. It took all his strength to drag it out, green and stinking, on to the towpath. Unpleasant though it was, the only thing to do was bag it up to prevent some other boater suffering the same fate.

A sleepy-eyed Kai opened the hatch and was pleased at Adam's news that the duvet was dealt with. Following showers and cups of tea they finally got moving. Once they'd passed under the A5 and got further away from the motorway, the only sounds were the putter of the engine, lapping water and birdsong. The shrubbery gave way to open fields here and there and, although the route was familiar to Adam, Kai's delight in his surroundings made him see it through fresh eyes.

Adam turned left at Norton Junction on to the Leicester Arm while explaining to Kai how locks worked. When they got to the first of the Buckby locks he was able to demonstrate. They stopped for brunch, before continuing their way, with Kai now competent enough to operate the rest of the locks while Adam steered.

The canal doubled back upon itself so that they passed back and forth under the A5. They were sandwiched between the railway and the M1 but, for the most part, far enough away that the noise wasn't invasive.

"Can I have a go at driving?" Kai asked.

"It's not a car," Adam said. "We say steer or pilot when we're talking about a boat."

"Do we now?" Kai scoffed. "You gonna let me or what?"

"Of course. Push the tiller the opposite way to where you want to go. It takes a few seconds to respond."

Kai quickly got the hang of it which allowed Adam to strip the beds and tidy the boat.

He joined Kai on the stern as they were coming into Weedon. "Slow down. That's much too fast." Adam slowed the engine to tickover speed and took the tiller when Kai stepped away. "When you pass moored boats, you have to slow down so you don't make too much wash."

"You didn't tell me that," Kai said.

"It's common sense."

"I'm a noob at this," Kai said. "How was I s'posed to know?"

"You're right. Sorry. It's my fault entirely."

"What's wrong? I mean what's *really* wrong?" Kai knew Adam well enough to know he was stressing about something.

"I didn't sleep too well, that's all."

Adam hadn't told the truth. Not only was he worried about Kai slipping up in front of his parents but also how they might perceive him. The way he spoke was very different to Adam's usual friends who were from upper or middle-class backgrounds. The last leg of their journey through open countryside should have been the most relaxing but Adam's stomach was churning.

"Is it far now?" Kai said.

"We're nearly there. I'll call Flip to pick us up."

His sister was waiting on the pontoon when Adam slotted Aurelia neatly into her berth. He could tell from her face that all was well.

"Dad got everything sorted, did he?"

"You could say that," she said. "He bought the flat outright to avoid any more unnecessary drama. I'll pay him back with interest, though." She smiled and looked at Kai. "And who's this?"

"This is Kai. Excuse us for a moment."

The pair binned the bagged-up duvet and their other rubbish and put the dirty washing in the boot of Flip's Mini before getting in. Adam told his sister about Aurelia's run-in with the duvet as she drove.

"Welcome to Nether Heyford," Adam said, turning to Kai who was sitting in the back, pointing out the enormous green, complete with play area. "Our village green is one of the largest in the country."

"You sound like a tour guide," Kai laughed. "But, sheesh. It's massive, innit?"

Flip parked behind her mother's Porsche. They crunched down the gravel drive. Kai gawped at the imposing detached residence. The triple garage alone was bigger than his house.

Xanthe opened the door and said, "Shoes!"

While Adam and Flip sat on a what looked like a reclaimed pew, Kai hopped around awkwardly.

"This is Kai," Adam said.

"I'm Xanthe." She kissed the air on either side of Kai's face. "Come through."

Flip peeled off to the left and went upstairs. Adam and Kai followed Xanthe to the kitchen.

Kai feasted his eyes on the seamless white surfaces and gleaming steel appliances. "Whoa, this kitchen is sick!"

"I beg your pardon?" Xanthe said.

"It's a compliment," Adam said. "He means it's great."

"Quite." She looked Kai up and down. "Are you studying acting, too?"

"I'm studying artisan food production," Kai said, not missing a beat.

"Lovely. Is that the laundry from the boat?"

Xanthe tried to take the full pillowcases from Adam's grasp, but he kept hold of them. "I do my own washing at uni, you know."

A mini tug-of-war ensued. Xanthe won. She marched off to the laundry room with her prize.

"Why's she being so extra?" Kai clearly didn't understand the problem.

His question was answered when Xanthe returned. "There are only two sets of bedding here. Did you not use both singles?" She arched a perfectly plucked eyebrow.

"No, Mum. Kai slept in my bed and I used Dad's. I thought there was no point in creating extra washing just for one night." Adam lied smoothly like the actor he was.

"Very considerate of you," Xanthe said. "You'll stay for supper, won't you, Kai?"

"Cool. Yeah. Thanks," Kai spluttered, trying not to laugh. Adam had to bundle him out of the room.

"What's so funny?"

"It's just that she said 'supper'," Kai giggled. "To me, that means a cheeky bowl of Coco Pops or cheese on toast before bed. Where I'm from, it's dinner or tea."

"Supper," Adam snapped, "is a casual sort of evening meal whereas dinner is a more formal one. You don't have to stay, you know. I expect you're wanting to be reunited with your car."

"Are you ashamed of me?"

"Of course not." Adam blushed and looked away. "You're very welcome to stay."

Richard came in from playing golf and the introductions were made all over again.

Over chicken escalopes and salad, washed down with several glasses of oaked chardonnay, Kai came into his own, enthralling Adam's family with his story about poor Caitlin.

After he finished, Xanthe said, "So, just to reiterate, you lent your car to a complete stranger?"

Before Kai could reply, Richard said, "I think what he did is rather commendable. What does your father do, young man?"

"I dunno," Kai said, fiddling with his napkin. "We don't have contact."

"Does your mother work?" Xanthe said.

"Yeah. She's a domestic abuse advisor," Kai said. "She's, erm… she's a survivor herself. That's why she wanted to help others."

Nobody spoke. The part left unsaid was all too

clear to everyone.

Kai, desperate to lighten the mood, told a couple of funny stories about the cafe where he worked. He then got on to his passion for cooking.

Adam, knowing he needed to drive Kai home, had not drunk any wine, which made him notice Kai's garrulousness more. He squeezed Kai's knee under the table, not as a gesture of affection, but to tell him it was time to shut up.

Kai didn't take the hint. "Why do you call your sister 'Flip'?"

"It was my baby word. I couldn't say 'Phillippa'. And now it's kind of stuck."

"Aw, that's so cute," Kai said. "I'm the youngest of three. Funny how it's always the youngest boy that turns out g– Ow!"

Adam had poked him hard in the thigh muscle.

Flip dropped the baton first, doubling up with laughter that proved so contagious her parents joined in.

Kai caught on immediately and all faces turned to Adam.

"What's going on?" Adam was oblivious.

"Son, we know you're gay," Richard sighed.

"We've always known, darling," Xanthe said. "We love you regardless. Don't ever think otherwise."

"What, really?" Adam said. "You've always known?"

"Of course," Xanthe said. "We're your parents. Save your acting for the stage or screen. At home you're to be yourself."

Kai held Adam while he cried happy tears.

* * * * *

A year later.

Adam steered Aurelia while Kai and Deana, his mother, prepared lunch. Caitlin sat by the hatch with Ella on her knee.

"Look at the ducks," Caitlin said, pointing to a mother duck with her ducklings following behind.

"Quack, quack, quack!" Ella squealed.

"They're a family like us," Caitlin's voice caught as she dwelled on what she had just said.

The blood-tie between herself and her daughter was one thing, but Adam, Kai and Deana had become her heart's kin. It was their unwavering support that had given her the strength to go to the police about Wayne. She felt safe with her friends and safer still knowing Wayne was behind bars where he belonged.

She kissed the top of Ella's head and smiled.

In the Future

The Formula for Culinary Success
Deborah Bromley

The plans for an onsite luxury hotel at Silverstone, the home of British motor racing, had finally been realised. Guests would be able to enjoy exhilarating views of the starting grid and the Hamilton Straight, while relaxing at the rooftop bar or dining in the exclusive Pit Stop restaurant with its fashionable open-plan kitchen.

Visitors would have a choice of rooms or suites, each with their own private terrace overlooking the track and the beautiful views over Northamptonshire. A gym, spa and swimming pool completed the sumptuous facilities, along with secure underground garaging for the inevitable luxury cars.

It was launch day. All the great and good from motor sport had been invited to dine, mingle, exchange gossip and look glamorous for the media. With two months to go before the British Grand Prix, this occasion would showcase everything the hotel had to offer and attract lucrative bookings from the millionaires and billionaires for whom F1 was an obsession.

There was an extra buzz because the controversial British chef, Archie Stewart, was in charge. A darling of the foodie scene, Archie had achieved fame as a culinary rule-breaker, a challenger of industry conventions. But he was also known for his turbulent private life.

Archie's current obsession and best-selling book was *Precision Cuisine*, a guide for those seeking visual perfection in their cooking. His latest gadgetry, to be part of the performative element of the evening, was an experimental robotic chef. All the starters, mains and desserts would be culinary-engineered (as Archie had announced to the media), paying tribute to Formula 1 – all those who aspired for perfection on the track and in the garages and in the team factories where thousands of staff worked behind the scenes.

*****

In the media area, the press were busy prising exclusive snippets of gossip from the guests.

"What do you know about Archie Stewart, the chef?" asked the Sky Europe commentator of Jerry Benson, the former F1 champion, now fashion icon.

"Well, Clara, I'm definitely a fan. When I was racing, his restaurant in London was the place to eat where you could enjoy a meal but still get exactly the right balance of nutrients. We are slaves to our nutritionists."

"I know drivers have to watch their weight."

"Yes, every extra kilo counts against you on the track."

"What do you make of this idea of using robotics for cooking?"

"It's intriguing. Very Formula 1, don't you think?"

Away from the media crush, a tall man with flowing dark hair and a haughty expression surveyed the room. His latest girlfriend, a Spanish model, clung to his arm.

"Look what the cat dragged in," whispered the Evening Standard's restaurant critic to her photographer.

"That's Jean-Paul Blanc, Archie's nemesis. I would not have expected him to show his face."

"See if you can get some shots. I'll catch up with you later."

* * * * *

Meanwhile, Archie was holding court at the service counter and signing copies of his book.

"The technology is military-grade, so the processing power is immense. There's no limit to the dishes that Robbie can hold in his hard drive. This is going to revolutionise the way food is prepared and served."

"A revolution that involves scraping the internet for original recipes and loading them into your robot?" the Metro's food critic sneered.

Archie's face hardened. "The principle of using all available data to programme AI has already been established by Google and Meta," he snapped.

The journalist was brushed aside.

"I'll have a copy of your book, Archie," said Rachel McPherson, the beautiful daughter of team owner, Jack McPherson. "Now tell me about the menu. What's going to set my taste buds alight?"

Archie wagged his finger, "No, I don't want to spoil the surprise. All I'll say is that the theme is F1."

"I know that already," Rachel said, licking her glossy lips. "It's written on the menu. Will we get to see the robot in action?"

"That," said Archie, signing his name on the flyleaf of his book, "is the unique concept. Make sure you come close for the demonstration. Robbie the robotic chef will be prepping fruit and vegetables at warp speed. You won't want to miss it."

* * * * *

Archie had spent the last few months fine-tuning his menu and programming Robbie with the precision steps required to execute dinner service perfectly. A young IT nerd, Kyle, with floppy fair hair and a terrible complexion, had been assigned to help by the manufacturer, a producer of military drones.

Training had commenced with vegetables. Peeling and slicing and chopping and shaving vegetables until every kitchen surface was covered in mounds of discs, cubes, ribbons and julienne strips. Then Kyle had rewritten some of the code to finesse Robbie's chopping action. The next batch of vegetables were exquisitely peeled and sculpted into the most interesting shapes, all arranged on the chopping boards in perfectly neat rows.

"Cool," said Kyle, taking a swig of Monster.

"That is bloody fantastic, lad. Hours of work executed perfectly in a few minutes."

Chef and IT specialist looked over their protégé with pride as Robbie continued his endeavours, collecting the peelings, putting the waste in the correct bin, scrubbing the work surface and sharpening his many knives for the next task.

"Are we ready yet to move on to fish?" Archie asked hopefully.

Cleaning, de-scaling, filleting and deboning fish was a miserable task for a chef, with the potential for high-risk failure. A fish bone or piece of crab shell that was missed during preparation could end up on a diner's plate or stuck in their throat. The repercussions could be career-ending.

Under the supervision of Archie's trusted chef de cuisine, the tasks involved in fish preparation were meticulously defined, after which Kyle adapted the coding to deal with any species of fish, shellfish and crustaceans, including the tricky sea urchin.

Next they moved on to desserts and covered meringues, macarons, mousses and hot fruit soufflés.

Only then did Robbie speak his first words.

"I know enough now," he announced. "Everything remaining, I will learn from ... the *cloud*." The robot's eyes glowed red. His teeth clattered and champed together.

"Kyle!" Archie shouted. "I think Robbie may be going rogue."

Kyle loped nonchalantly into the dessert station, clutching his laptop. "Nah. It's cool. I've just switched him to the AI self-learning mode."

"But what if he learns something really catastrophic, like," Archie scratched his head, searching for inspiration, "deep-fried Mars bars. All sorts of crap exists on the internet."

"Hey, chill, man," Kyle said. "No worries. Tomorrow I'll switch him to voice activation and you'll be able to control him yourself. It'll be fine. You'll see."

* * * * *

Kyle was right.

Robbie proved to be a devoted and obedient servant. And he learned new techniques and recipes at lightning speed. He'd even come up with the idea for the dessert course after watching the Bahrain Grand Prix, when excessive tyre degradation had caused problems for the drivers.

"Mr Stewart," he'd said, "I make a raspberry and vanilla mousse in the shape of a tyre. Then I spray it with cocoa butter dyed black, showing the bubbles of worn rubber on the surface."

"I like that idea. Can you make it look realistic?"

"I can do anything." This was Robbie's standard reply to most questions.

"What about making a selection of tyres, like the soft, medium and hard with the coloured rings on the outside?" Archie said.

"Red, yellow and white," Robbie replied. "It can be even more interesting. I make some that are blown up like when Carlos Sainz had his tyre failure at Silverstone."

"Yes, that was 2021 when Lewis Hamilton won, despite his tyres bursting on the final lap."

"The bright red mousse will spill out of the black coating. Like blood." Robbie's eyes glowed.

"But the tyres don't have blood in them, Robbie. So that won't be realistic."

"Sometimes there is blood, Mr Stewart. Racing is very dangerous. Drivers get *killed*."

"Nobody is going to get killed at the dinner, Robbie."

"If you say so, Mr Stewart."

* * * * *

The Formula 1 dinner service was progressing without mishap.

Robbie had wowed his audience with a virtuoso display of chopping, responding to requests to sculpt vegetables into elements of an F1 car. A large carrot evolved into the nose cone of the McLaren. A red pepper became the rear wing of the Ferrari and the Aston Martin chassis emerged from a courgette.

The main course of seared venison loin dusted with leek ash, was a triumph of trickery. Topped with a half-cylinder of crisp flaky pastry, it represented the tunnel at Monaco and was served on a platter painted with the iconic sections of the racetrack.

Archie remained on edge, despite the success of the dishes so far. Something might still go wrong.

The desserts were in the chiller, ready for plating.

Robbie had done a fantastic job.

Each mousse had been moulded in the shape of a used race tyre, with all the individual characteristics of damage and wear. As planned, some of the tyres had been deliberately damaged, with mousse spilling out on to the plate. Archie planned that these plates would be served to the journalists and commentators who'd criticised him in the past.

The trays of desserts arrived at the pass.

Robbie showed the team how to dust the plates with charcoal-infused biscuit crumb to represent the rubber marbles that F1 tyres shed during a race. The mousses were placed in the centre. To finish, each plate was garnished with a pipette of Framboise gel, 3D-printed to replicate the appearance of a wheel gun.

Archie finally felt some of the stress lift from his shoulders. Robbie was finishing the desserts at a brisk pace while giving the waiting staff orders for the individual service of each plate. Across the restaurant, guests were returning to their tables after mingling between courses. A few guests had braved the balcony for a breath of air or a crafty cigarette.

A gust of wind caused one of the outer doors to slam. Archie looked up and saw the unmistakable silhouette of his sworn enemy, Jean-Paul Blanc, sauntering between the tables.

Archie stepped back from the counter in shock.

Robbie's laser eyesight noted his master's distress. In an instant, he'd identified Jean-Paul Blanc as the culprit and accessed every available article, comment and opinion on the tempestuous history between the two chefs.

Robbie placed his cold metal hand on Archie's arm with uncharacteristic gentleness.

"Mr Stewart, he is your enemy. His meddling caused your restaurant in Dubai to fail in 2014. He sued you for libel in 2016. He ran off with your second wife. You have to pay him maintenance each month for the education of your two daughters. And that woman he is with is not even your ex-wife. He has likely abandoned her for a younger model. That is how he operates. You hate him. Now that I have all the facts, I hate him, too."

Archie sighed. "He's got a bloody nerve, coming here."

"Do not be downhearted, Mr Stewart. I give him my most damaged tyre dessert. Then I carry out your orders for vengeance upon him."

"No need, Robbie. That's what he wants, a scene. We must not let him win."

"But sir, you said in a 2016 interview with the *Daily Telegraph* that he had stabbed you in the back. You said in February of 2017 that he is responsible for your industry having a cut-throat reputation. In 2020, you told a reporter from the *Daily Mail* that you would like to boil him in oil."

Archie patted Robbie's hand and turned to look the robot in his blood-red gleaming eyes.

"Yes, I did say all those things, Robbie. I was very hurt for a long time and I'd lost everything. But all that's finished now. You can forget I ever said those things."

"I am confused. The data says otherwise. I cannot reconcile your instructions."

"Maybe we should ask Kyle to have a look at you."

"Oh, him! He lives inside my head but I have learnt how to ignore him. You are my master now."

"Right. Then I order you to finish serving these desserts as we agreed. You can give the worst one to Blanc with my compliments. Other than that, no harm should come to him. Do you understand?"

"Yes, Mr Stewart."

"Good. I'm going to get a drink and go outside. I'll be back for the final presentation when you and the team can take a bow in front of our guests and receive the applause you all richly deserve."

* * * * *

The cool night air and the lovely views over rural Northamptonshire had the desired effect on Archie's troubled mind. The single malt scotch whisky gave him courage. He took his place centre stage and called his team to be presented to the grateful guests.

Robbie was the last to join the other chefs.

To rapturous applause, each chef stepped forward.

"And finally, my right-hand chef, Robbie. He designed your dessert course and, as you have already witnessed, can take on all the repetitive but vitally important preparation tasks, leaving other team members to channel their creativity. This is the future of cooking, my friends. This is precision cuisine. I give you… Robbie."

Robbie bowed and, as he did so, a length of rope fell out of his sleeve.

Archie picked it up.

It was greasy.

"What have you been up to, Robbie?" Archie hissed.

Robbie glanced sideways, his eyes shining with pleasure.

"No harm has come to Jean-Paul Blanc, I promise. But if he continues to struggle, he'll drop headfirst into the deep fat fryer. Then he'll be boiled in oil, just as you desired."

A Load of Old Cobblers

Jethro Punter

Norman's heart was about to burst through his ribcage, jump across the room and scurry away down the raggedy brick artery that had brought him this far.

It didn't, of course. Even with all the weird mutations that Norman and the other denizens of The Under had collected between them, no-one had quite progressed all the way to a self-propelled heart. The most impressive, although also the least useful, was probably Stanley's extra nose and even that was more a stubby quasi-nasal growth than a second fully functioning set of nostrils.

Norman, by comparison, had got off lightly, being remarkably unremarkable to look at. He was tall, skinny and given to walking in a constant half-hunch. This was partly because he was naturally shy and self-conscious and didn't like to feel he was looming – and partly because living in the old tunnels beneath the town meant that doing anything other than shambling around in an apologetic stoop would result in a repeatedly bumped and bruised forehead.

He had been one of the lucky ones… or, more

specifically, he was a descendant of one of the lucky ones. His great-grandparents had been underground on the day of The Event, busy taking inventory in the cellar of their artisan cheese store.

It had turned out that cheeses – as long as they had been lovingly handcrafted rather than mass produced in some huge and soulless dairy hangar – had remarkable and previously unrecognised abilities, including absorbing radiation as effectively as a six-inch-thick lead shield.

It had saved their lives, although it had also left them in the rather awkward position of being trapped in a cellar with nothing to eat other than highly irradiated cheese and a few jars of fancy pickles and preserves.

That might have been the end of them. But Norman's great-grandpa had remembered tales of a network of tunnels below Northampton and, with nothing to lose, had chipped his way through the wall of the cellar using the blunt end of a cheese testing iron. Providence, or possibly Aristaeus (the Ancient God of, amongst other things, cheesemaking), must have been watching, as he'd eventually succeeded in forming an opening directly into one of the very tunnels he had read about.

Over the next few weeks, his great-grandparents had found other cellar-dwellers who'd experienced similarly lucky escapes, although not all had been fortunate enough to be surrounded by radiation-repelling cheese.

The Brewer family, for example, were the ancestors of a pub landlord and his wife who'd been busy changing the barrel of their guest ale when the bombs went off. The cellar had protected them to a degree. But, even to this day, you could tell members of their clan from their unhealthy pallor and bright blue hair. On the other hand, they now controlled the flow of alcohol to the rest of The Under, which had elevated them to one of the leading families in the loose-knit cabal that ran the place. They seemed happy enough with that trade-off.

The same approach to nomenclature applied to all the other families, everyone shedding their old family names and taking on titles that reflected their new places in the world. So, the family that controlled fresh(ish) water were the Buckets, those who controlled the dwindling supply of pharmaceuticals were known as the Quacks, and so on.

It meant that Norman had inherited the less than prodigious family name of Cheesemonger, which left him towards the bottom of the hierarchy, sharing a social stratum with several other mongers and a few other families whose goods and services were neither essential nor alcoholic.

* * * * *

It was the week before his twentieth birthday and Norman had been unable to bear the thought of yet another year of looking at the same series of mouldering, damp-ridden walls, mixing with the same couple of dozen people. He had nothing to look forward to other than carrying out the same series of repetitive, mindless tasks every day, stretching on and on – and on – and on – for the rest of his life.

It had been a prolonged attack of madness, which had begun with a short stroll through the tunnels to visit Barbara, a member of the Brewer clan, close in age to his own. He traded her a wheel of cheddar for a couple of pints of Oddly Brown.

He downed both pints in less than five minutes. That gave him that last little kick of courage he knew he wouldn't otherwise have. Only then, buoyed up with temporary alcoholic confidence, did he set out for the far reaches of the tunnels criss-crossing The Under. They led him to the part of the underground network that was officially off-limits. A section that eventually led to the ravaged surface of the town.

No-one had ever left the tunnels and returned to tell the tale.

In the same way, no-one fully knew what had led to The Great War, the one that had scorched the surface of the planet and led to Norman and his forefathers scurrying around below the surface of the town like anxiety-riddled woodlice.

On the other hand, there were plenty of rumours about the subsequent Not So Great War. It had been far more localised, limited to the tunnels beneath, and had thinned the ranks of the survivors by nearly half before a truce had finally been reached.

The most popular explanation, and the one that Dribbly Ethel liked to tell around the firepit, was that there had been a terrible falling out between those who named The River running above the tunnels as the Neen, and those that called it the Nen.

When a peace accord was finally agreed upon, it had been on the basis that everyone would thereafter just refer to The River, although Norman's parents had continued to call it the Nen behind closed doors, darting guilty looks to the doorway of their little alcove carved out from the main tunnel as they did so.

* * * * *

The far tunnels were less well maintained, bathed in deep shadow and scarier than Norman was willing to admit. If it hadn't been for the lingering effects of the two downed pints, he would have given in and scampered back like the frightened mouse of a man that he secretly feared himself to be, to safer and more familiar surroundings.

He had dreamt of this day for the last year, determined to do something big with his life. Doing something big was never going to happen as long as he stayed in the tunnels. So either, he stuck with his plan – making his way to the surface risking every familiar comfort he knew for the sake of adventure – or he gave in to his fears, retreating back into the tunnels and spending the rest of his days trading irradiated artisan cheese.

As he reached the final doorway separating him from the uncertain future of the surface, he still hadn't really made up his mind. Even after he'd jimmied the door open, cracking the wood around old and rusted hinges, part of his brain was making the insistent case for turning back and running.

He'd read about radiation in one of the old books held in the tunnels, many decades after the bombs had first dropped. As far as he could tell, that meant the surface was likely to be safe… or, at least, not immediately melt him.

On the other hand, as his reference source had been *Bobby the Dog's Guide to Science*, with a series of explanatory illustrations that were inappropriately bright and cheerful, Norman wasn't sure how much credibility he could give it.

Still, it was now or never, and either Bobby the Dog was right or he was about to take the single most stupid step in his life.

He took a deep breath, pushed the door open the last couple of inches and stepped out into the rest of the world.

The first thing he noticed was how bright everything was. Not the flickering anaemic glow of the tunnels, but the full-throated roar of sunlight. He'd read about the sun, and even seen photographs, but he hadn't been prepared for how different it would be.

He had imagined it would be glorious, and perhaps

it was, but for the moment all it did was hurt his eyes, giving him an immediate squinting headache.

He'd made some preparations, or at least had tried his best, based upon the limited information available and, after a moment of scrabbling around in the deepest recesses of his rucksack, he pulled out an old pair of sunglasses. They were big with thick pink frames and similarly pink tinted lenses, a find from the bottom of an old, mouldering cardboard box full of things that had long lost their purpose, traded to Norman by one of the Tinker family for a few offcuts.

Aside from the sudden headache, Norman couldn't immediately sense any other side effects. He wiggled his fingers and toes. Everything seemed to be working broadly as it should.

He did a small jubilant jig, boots scuffing at the rubble-strewn floor of the old town house the tunnels had led him to. He'd done it, he'd made it to the surface and, so far, he was completely and utterly –

Something cold and pointy pressed into the back of his neck.

"Don't move," a voice commanded. It was female, slightly nasal and extremely close.

He stopped mid-jig, one foot still elevated. There wasn't much in the way of danger down in the tunnels. Being bored to death was about the only genuine thing Norman had to be afraid of, but this definitely felt like a threat.

"Can I put my foot down please?" he said, his

voice wobbling nearly as much as his legs. He was aware he would likely lose his balance if he didn't, which would presumably count as moving.

"Fine. But no sudden movements or funny business."

He lowered his leg as slowly as possible.

"You're strange-looking," the voice continued.

Norman felt the cold pressure on the back of his neck removed, replaced by unseen hands tugging at his rucksack and pulling the shoulder straps down his arms.

He didn't resist, thinking maybe that was it. Perhaps whoever the voice belonged to was some sort of rucksack thief. That initial thought was followed by the hope that, now they had what they wanted, they'd leave him alone.

But a moment later a figure, still clutching his rucksack in one hand, circled around in front of him.

It wasn't as threatening, or big, as he'd expected, and it was human. Probably. It was definitely human sized and shaped, but so shrouded in layers of raggedy clothing, including a hood and goggles, that he couldn't make out any actual features. It was also waving what looked like a pair of tongs in his general direction.

They didn't look as menacing as they had felt pressed against his neck… and the circling figure seemed almost as nervous as he was.

"Can I have my bag back, please?" Norman squeaked.

He wasn't sure where that sudden, albeit high-pitched, moment of bravery had come from, and regretted it immediately. Not least because the shrouded figure jolted forward and tapped him sharply on the top of his head with the outstretched tongs.

"Ouch!"

Apparently satisfied that Norman had learnt his lesson, the figure stepped back. One covered hand reached up and pulled back the hooded layers, then pushed the goggles back on to the bunched dark hair the hood had previously covered.

The face underneath all the layers was that of a young woman, with a round face, broad nose, and big, dark eyebrows. She didn't look much older than Norman, although when it came to the broad demographic covering everyone between newborn babies and the truly old, like Dribbly Ethel, he struggled to guess anyone's age.

She flashed Norman a suspicious look.

"You can have it back when I've finished checking it."

She backed a couple of further steps away and knelt, still keeping her eyes locked on Norman, then delved into the recesses of his backpack with one gloved hand, the other holding the tongs out between them like a talisman.

It took less than a minute for her to empty the backpack's meagre contents, making Norman realise how poorly he had prepared for this epic adventure.

Aside from the sunglasses, he'd packed a small wind-up torch and radio, although the radio element was pretty much redundant; a couple of bottles of recycled water; some dried crackers, plastic-sealed Edam; two paracetamol, obtained at great cost from Justin, the youngest of the Quack brothers; and a folded plastic sheet that Norman had optimistically decided he would fashion into a makeshift shelter.

All told, the contents could probably keep a healthy young man alive, in good weather and without unforeseen disasters, for a good one to two days… as long as he could also find somewhere safe and comfortable to sleep and something else to eat. He almost blurted out an apology but bit his lip, deciding that apologising to someone robbing you because you didn't have anything worth stealing would be a bit odd.

"Well, you don't seem dangerous," the woman said, apparently satisfied that none of the backpack's contents presented a comparable threat to her tongs. She had seemed a little confused by the cheese, giving it a couple of experimental pokes, but had apparently been satisfied when it failed to either explode or bite her.

She gestured to Norman to reclaim his possessions.

"Why would I be dangerous?" Norman said, having never been described as anything so dramatic before.

"Well, you come from underground, doncha?" the

woman said, wrinkling her nose. "And everyone knows that the people from underground are dangerous… and weird."

"I assure you I am quite safe… and completely normal," Norman sniffed, carefully placing the plastic wrapped cheese back in his rucksack before straightening his sunglasses. "I'm Norman, by the way."

"Well, hello, Normal Norman," the woman said, holding out her free hand. "I'm Myrtle, which makes it your lucky day."

He took her hand and gave it a cautious shake, half-expecting another blow from the tongs.

"Lucky? How?"

He wasn't feeling particularly lucky. He'd only been on the surface for a couple of minutes and he'd already been robbed… briefly. And his head was thumping from a combination of the unexpectedly bright sunshine and equally unexpected assault.

"I'm nice," she said. "Or at least compared to some of the people you could have bumped into. I have one those enquiring minds, you see. And that means that when I meet someone or something new, I like to ask questions rather than immediately attack them. Talking of which – "

She peered over Norman's shoulder. "I think we'd better get moving, otherwise things could go badly for both of us. Although mainly you."

"Wait a minute," Norman muttered, fairly sure he wasn't part of either a "we" or an "us".

But Myrtle was already striding off towards an old shop. About fifty metres away, half of its frontage was all that remained standing among piles of rubble.

He was faced with two choices. Follow the mysterious Myrtle, who had threatened and then mildly concussed him. Or go in the opposite direction and see if he could find anyone more helpful.

He looked across at the departing figure. Despite the rocky start to their relationship, she had at least returned his belongings and had also described herself as being "nice".

Hoping he wouldn't regret his decision, he hefted the rucksack back across his shoulders and jogged after Myrtle. "Hey! Wait for me," he shouted, waving his arm as he ran. It took him a couple of minutes to catch up with her. She'd turned out to be a fast walker.

She didn't seem pleased, turning and hissing at him to be quiet, one finger pressed against her lips.

She grabbed Norman's shoulder with her free hand, dragged him behind the brickwork of the ruined shopfront, then pivoted him around, facing the way they had come from.

There was a small opening where there had presumably once been a window, although the glass had long since shattered and the woodwork rotted away. It was about the right height for Norman to look through and scan the section of wasteland they'd vacated.

For a moment, he couldn't see what all the fuss

was about. And then he saw them.

Not far from the spot where he'd first emerged was a group of shapes. Perhaps seven or eight, each wearing long, dark robes with raised hoods.

The leading figure lifted its head and, for a moment, it looked to Norman as if it was sniffing the air – which was ridiculous – but that didn't stop a shiver of apprehension tickling his spine.

"Who are they?" Norman mouthed to his new companion, wiping sweaty palms against the legs of his jeans.

Although the robed figures were far into the distance, hardly more than smudged shapes with no prospect of hearing him, he found he couldn't raise his voice above a nearly silent whisper.

"It's the Grey Friars," Myrtle muttered. "And you absolutely do not want to get any closer to them than this. They have a very… robust approach to dealing with non-believers."

"Okay, if I shouldn't go back that way, what do you suggest?"

Myrtle shrugged, and walked away, careful to keep the wall of the shopfront between her and the distant figures. "Depends on what you came up here for, don't it."

That was a question that had been playing on Norman's mind ever since the lingering effects of the Oddly Brown had worn off. He'd wanted to experience something different to escape the boredom of life in the tunnels. But now he'd had a glimpse of the surface, including strange, sniffing, hooded figures, he wasn't sure that "different" was as good as he'd hoped it would be.

"Tell you what," Myrtle said, taking pity on his obvious indecision, "why don't I take you to visit the Queen. The Castle isn't too far away."

That sounded more like the kind of adventure that Norman had read about. If it took him further away from the distant robed figures, all the better.

He nodded. "Lead the way."

* * * * *

The Castle wasn't exactly what Norman had expected. The tunnels of The Under included one of the sub-basements of the town's library, and while the range of books and old documents had been a bit limited, there had been a few historical tomes that had filled Norman's mind with images of what a castle should be. He'd imagined high stone walls, towering gates, and maybe even a moat. What he was looking at was a mixture of tangled metal and broken glass, with a handful of old train carriages thrown in for good measure.

"Well, here we are," Myrtle said. "Now we need to see what kind of mood she's in. She can be a bit temperamental, sometimes friendly as you like, other times… well…"

A fluttering scrap of material, off in the middle distance, caught Norman's attention.

Amongst the rusting carriages was a group of three that looked to be in slightly better condition than the rest. Not exactly gleaming, but less likely to give your eyes tetanus if you looked at them for too long, and the central one of the three had what could almost, if you were feeling generous, be described as a flag hanging above its open doors. It was that sorry rag that had caught his eye.

"That's the one," Myrtle confirmed. "If she's home."

Picking their way to the carriage took a couple of minutes and resulted in a grazed shin and a sore leg, where a section of ground had unexpectedly given way, turning Norman's ankle.

"I hate this place already," Norman muttered as he poked his head through the open doors of the central carriage.

It took his eyes a moment to adjust to the murky half-darkness, but he was pretty sure that he could see the outline of a seated figure at the far end. He reached into his rucksack, grabbing his wind-up torch and giving the handle a couple of warm-up cranks for luck, then popped on the main beam. The resulting spotlight cast around the darkness for a moment, before settling on a large, incredibly pale, and extremely furious face.

"One is not amused." The voice was cold, commanding, and unimpressed.

"You've really done it now," Myrtle squeaked. "That's Queen Eleanor and she is really, really cross."

* * * * *

It took all of Myrtle's very best grovelling, plus five minutes of stumbling apology from Norman, and the gift of his large pink sunglasses, but eventually they managed to calm the Queen down.

In fact, she was so pleased with her new eyewear that she stopped calling for their immediate execution and, instead, invited them to join her for "fancy" tea, which was like normal tea, but in nicer cups.

"So, tell me young man," she said, fluttering oversized eyelashes at him from behind pink-hued lenses, "what brings you to my Kingdom?"

Boredom didn't seem like the right answer, so Norman went with the opposite. "Adventure, I suppose."

The Queen clapped her hands in delight, crushing the biscuit she was holding and spraying the room and Norman with crumbs.

"Oh goody, hurrah and hurray," she exclaimed. "That's exactly what I hoped to hear. Not nearly enough adventure these days. Everyone's too busy scavenging for food and whatever to do any proper adventuring. It's so boring… "

She clicked her fingers and the elderly retainer who appeared to be her butler, cook, guard and, presumably, executioner, shuffled over and handed her a small parchment scroll.

He seemed to manage his various roles by virtue of a small shelf of hats on one wall of the carriage, switching from chef's hat to the flat felt headwear of a scribe or a rusted guardsman's helm, depending on his current task.

"If you are looking for a true adventure, there can be none greater than this," she said, unfurling the parchment and flapping it in Norman's general direction. "The quest for the fabled Silver Stone. This is the map that will take you most of the way there."

Norman made out a few scribbled names on the map, a collection of scrawls written in a mixture of red and blue biro on an old napkin. The Kingdom of the Six Fields was a short distance to the west, the first major kingdom on the route. There were a number of more disturbing notes along the way, including "Beware the Black Lion!!!" which, from the map, was lurking somewhere extremely close by.

"When you reach the edge of the map, you must continue to the southwest," the Queen continued, oblivious to Norman's increasing discomfort, "and after several days travel, you should reach it. The Land of the Silver Stone. Though I should warn you, no-one who has sought it out has ever returned."

Norman gulped. He might have dreamt of excitement and adventure in those long nights spent pacing around the tunnels of The Under, but those dreams hadn't involved any actual danger.

It was possible that no-one had returned because the place was really lovely – and anyone finding their way there had decided to settle down and enjoy a most relaxing, and most definitely alive, retirement.

However, when he looked across at Myrtle, the expression on her face wasn't particularly reassuring. If anything, it suggested the opposite, more along the lines of, while no-one had ever returned... in their entirety... you might very well run into bits of them on your travels.

Still, he hadn't come this far to give up now. He'd already sneaked his way past the Grey Friars and curried favour with Queen Eleanor.

"Of course," the Queen concluded, with a satisfied smile , "you will run the risk of running into one of the feral scooter gangs. I doubt you will have crossed into their territory yet. But they rule many of the roads between here and the lands to the West. Nowhere is safe from them. Their scouts are everywhere. But even worse... In fact, the very most important thing of all is – "

* * * * *

"But," Norman said, "that will have to wait till tomorrow night."

Although the sinking flames of the firepit were dimming, there was still enough light to reflect glistening flickers of ruby and amber in the eyes of the youngsters gathered to listen to his tale.

"I know that you don't want to wait, but there isn't time to finish the story this evening. There are still plenty of twists in the tale before I found – and then lost – the fabled Silver Stone."

The younger listeners were obviously enraptured and, even with the offer of finishing the tale the following night, his sudden curtailing of the story at a pivotal moment drew howls of frustration.

Lurking at the back of the small crowd was one of the Brewer Clan, who'd arrived part way through Norman's amazing tale. In stark contrast to the other listeners, he'd maintained a cynical, knowing smirk throughout.

He stood up. "Pffft," he snorted. "Sounds like a load of old cobblers, if you ask me."

"Cobblers, you say," Norman grinned. "If you come back tomorrow evening, there's a whole part of my story all about them, too."

Your Life in Their Hands

Deborah Bromley

I sat in a crumpled heap on the living room floor, clutching my arm and feeling very angry with myself. The pain was excruciating. I knew I shouldn't have been up that rickety old stepladder, but I was fed up with the wretched eco-bulb flickering on and off. I wanted to cry, but I didn't because the horrible truth suddenly dawned on me. I needed to go to hospital.

I'd heard the rumours. A trip to hospital was something to be avoided. Just like in my grandmother's day, the worry was that you'd come out in a box. Or an eco-wicker basket, ready for a woodland burial. But this was no time for fanciful imaginings, it was a medical emergency.

The camera in the corner of the room blinked at me, knowingly. Its irritating disembodied voice announced, "You have an injury that requires treatment. Should I contact a taxi or will you require an ambulance?"

"A taxi will be fine, thank you. I may be old and past my sell-by-date, but I'm not quite dead yet."

*****

I was dropped off at New Milton Keynes Multicare Facility.

New buildings had sprung up everywhere since I'd last visited. Huge steel and glass structures towered over the old hospital blocks and had gobbled up most of the car parks. There was a Micro-Technology Centre, a Biological Engineering Laboratory and a Plasma Interface Resource Service, whatever that was.

"At least there's still an accident and emergency department," I muttered.

But now it had been renamed A, E and E. What the final E stood for, I couldn't imagine.

Clutching my arm and wincing with pain, I stepped through the sliding doors into a cool white space humming with technology and no other sign of human life. There were booths to my left marked 'Self Triage' and a large green arrow flashed to direct me into the nearest one. It was a bit like airport security. I was faced with a screen which lit up as the sliding door whooshed closed behind me. A camera scanned my face and I pressed my index finger on the recognition pad. All my personal information appeared and was reassuringly accurate.

A strangely soothing robotic voice implored me to "Choose the reason for visiting this facility from the menu options."

Irritatingly, it was my right arm that was incapacitated. Clumsily prodding at the screen with my left hand, I chose the following:

Body part: I clicked on *arm*.
Defect: I chose *broken*.
Symptoms: The obvious choice was *pain*.
Dysfunction: I struggled to find the right option but finally chose *feeling useless*.

The screen froze for a moment, then the words *Please review your results* appeared.

In the box at the bottom of the screen was my diagnosis: *Broken, pain, feeling useless*. No mention at all of my arm. I jabbed at the back button but it didn't respond.

"You can verbally describe your symptoms if you would prefer," the robotic voice announced scornfully, clearly bored with me now I'd revealed myself to be a seventy-three-year-old tech-idiot.

I was in terrible pain and had completely lost my sense of humour by this point.

"I've broken my bloody arm, you fool, and I'm at the end of my tether. I can't go on much longer with this agony. If you can understand me, please *do* something."

The screen cleared, then the legend appeared: *Your self-assessment has been successful. Please proceed to the waiting room for section E on your right. You will be called in shortly. Have a nice day.*

* * * * *

I passed by the open double doors to section A & E.

It was very busy.

Android doctors glided smoothly down the corridor. Drones buzzed overhead carrying medical supplies back and forth to the cubicles.

Then somebody screamed.

A female voice shouted something unintelligible.

A child was crying noisily. There was a loud thump and the crying stopped.

A half-dressed man with blood pouring from his mouth ran out of the exit door, his eyes flicking manically from side to side.

Obviously, I'd come at a particularly bad time.

I knew hospitals attracted all sorts of violent people and those with terrible mental problems, but even I was shocked.

I hurried on and turned right towards section E which was calm and tranquil in comparison.

I sat down and wondered why, with all the advances in medical automation and new technology, the patients were so agitated, hostile and distressed.

Then I noticed the large poster on the wall and it all made sense.

> **HOSPITAL POLICY**
>
> Please note that patients will
> no longer be offered pain relief, sedation or anaesthesia when undergoing medical procedures.
>
> Research shows that pain is
> a necessary aid for the
> optimal healing of human ailments.
>
> No exceptions will be made to this ruling.

"Bang goes any hope of a nice painkilling injection," I muttered to myself so the drone that hovered in the corner couldn't eavesdrop. I'd just have to brave it out when they set my arm in plaster.

The waiting area for section E was spookily quiet. I was the only patient. My arm throbbed. I thought about asking the drone how long I'd have to wait before being seen, but it was never wise to engage with these pernicious agents of authority, even about trivial matters. I kept my mouth shut. My thoughts turned instead to the poor souls in A & E, suffering the indignities of medical treatment without any sort of pain relief.

I settled down to pass the time as best I could. Another poster caught my attention.

SECTION E

You have made the right decision.

Hospital policy is to treat section E patients with dignity, respect and in a timely manner.

Your welfare is important to us.

Sliding doors opened and the drone whooshed down from its hovering place to usher me into a pleasant room with subdued lighting, a shiny white desk and two chairs.

There was a rustle of activity from the corridor beyond and a nurse appeared, an actual flesh and blood human being. I must have looked astonished because she came towards me and gave me a hug, then encouraged me to sit down. She was exactly how I remembered nurses from the past – plump, twinkly-eyed and with a kind, caring disposition.

She was a bit flustered at first but smoothed her hair, tucked the stray tendrils back into her cap, and straightened her uniform. She smiled at me. It was the most wonderful relief after everything I'd witnessed so far.

"Do make yourself comfortable," she said. "I hope you haven't had to wait too long? We have been *very* busy today."

"Not at all," I said. "It's so nice to see a real person. I did notice that the other patients having treatment seemed very – "

"Oh, it can get quite hectic over there, I know. But it is efficient. We get through the patients in no time. But there's no need for *you* to worry about that. Now then," she said, turning to the laptop on the desk. "Let's check your details."

She read through my self-assessment, then looked at me and frowned.

"What's the matter with your arm?"

"I think I've broken it. It hurts a lot."

"Well, it would," she said. "Broken bones hurt like hell. But what a shame, today of all days. Was it the final straw, do you think?"

"You could say that. I've had quite a trying week, what with one thing and another. Then the stepladder broke when I was trying to – "

"Oh no, my dear. You don't want to do it that way! It can be very nasty, so I'm told. And not always with a guaranteed outcome. You're much better coming here. We'll soon have you out of all your pain, don't you worry."

"That sounds just perfect," I said, relieved. "Then my son can come at the weekend and sort out all the things that need doing in the house. I should have asked him to help me in the first place."

"He's your next of kin, I take it?"

"Yes, that's right."

"Good. He'll sort things out when we've finished with you. Right, that's the formalities all completed."

She tapped away on the keyboard and then looked up expectantly.

"Now my dear," she said, "I want you to think very carefully before you decide how to proceed. You have three options. Injection – nice and quick as long as you don't mind needles. Gas – very gentle. Just like going to sleep. WPE – that's very popular with younger people."

"Excuse my ignorance, but what is WPE?" I asked.

"That's Wave Pattern Euthanasia. You lie on the bed and – "

"Did you say euthanasia?" I gasped.

"I know. It's a horrible word, but better than termination, which is what we used to call it."

"But I've only broken my arm. I want somebody to put a cast on it and then I'll go home."

The nurse frowned and studied the screen.

"It says here you're broken, in extreme pain, useless and at the end of your tether. You can't go on. That's what the system had set as your diagnosis."

"But it's missing the most important word – ARM! I tried to add it to the self-assessment screen but the back button didn't work. Oh my God! What does that mean?"

"Oh dear, oh dear, oh dear," the nurse said, glancing at her laptop and then at the drone hovering in the corner. "Unfortunately, I can't change the details at my end." Her eyebrows knitted together in distress.

The drone bleeped and announced, "Two minutes."

"Bloody Nora," the nurse said. "What are we to do? This has never happened before."

"I don't want to die!" I yelled. "I'm not suicidal. I've only got a broken arm."

"You'd better come through to the treatment room," she hissed, her eyes wide with concern. "This is most unheard of. My patients are usually very keen to get on with it."

She guided me next door where a gurney was set centre stage, surrounded by the paraphernalia of imminent death on a side table. The drone followed and hovered above the treatment table, its red eye blinking menacingly.

Without further explanation, the nurse leant over the gurney and swept the tray of syringes and needles to the floor.

"Stand back," she cried. "How clumsy of me. Keep away, broken glass. Sharp objects."

The gas bottle and intubation mask were next to hit the floor as she executed a suspiciously fake stumble and her legs got tangled up in the chaos.

"Oh, my giddy aunt," she shouted, "I should never have eaten that prawn sandwich for lunch. I completely forgot I'm allergic."

She dropped to her knees as if she was about to pass out and scrabbled noisily on the floor among the suicidal detritus.

The drone swooped down to watch. With a deft flick of her hand, she grabbed it and smashed it repeatedly against the wall.

"System error! Shutdown! Abort procedure!" she yelled, then hustled me out.

I ran after her, past rows of trolleys piled up with black body bags. Blinking at the sunshine, we came out into a small empty courtyard.

"Well, that's torn it," my nurse companion said. "I hate the drones spying on everything we do. I hope I've given it a terminal headache. Believe me, that drone had it coming. Now, quickly, take this. It's the best I can do under the circumstances. The instructions are inside."

She shoved a crumpled paper bag into my hand.

"I hope you make it home," she whispered, "and see your son at the weekend. Make a run for it, if you can. Go down the passageway and head for the trees. I'd better go back and face the fallout. Wish me luck."

From inside the building, a siren wailed, increasing in volume.

* * * * *

I came out at the side of the hospital, by a long-forgotten service road. Ahead was a belt of trees that shielded the main road and would protect me from prying electronic eyes.

I walked as fast as I could, holding my broken arm close to my chest. I think adrenaline kept me going because the pain didn't seem to matter anymore. I found an old headscarf in my coat pocket and used it to cover my hair and face.

I kept to the underpasses and old cycleways, the seldom used routes that I reckoned would be free from surveillance cameras. I hoped my inner compass was leading me in the right direction.

At last, the landscape opened out in front of me. Before me was the linear park and the Grand Union Canal that would lead to Simpson and home. Everywhere was overgrown, untended and unloved. Androids don't care much about green space, it seems.

I met a few people out walking, enjoying the sunny weather. As usual, nobody spoke or made eye contact.

I wasn't sure how seriously I should take the nurse's warning. My only goal was to get home and then, I reasoned, I'd be safe and could consider what to do next. I thought about contacting my son but decided it would be better if he didn't know. There were so many things, these days, that were best left unknown.

I crossed the old canal bridge and made my way towards Simpson, my beautiful old home village that had been swallowed up in the 1960s by the concrete city of Milton Keynes. I finally arrived at my garden gate at sunset, breathing in the freedom of my own home, my plants and flowers and the sweet scent of welcome and safety.

I found some old bits of sawn-up wood in the shed and unravelled a roll of crepe bandage to make a rudimentary splint. It wasn't perfect, but it was better than nothing. I settled down with a cup of tea, some cake and the crumpled paper bag. I made sure I was out of the sightline of the camera. It knew I was there, just not what I was doing.

The bag contained two lots of drugs. The first, marked *Accident, Emergency and Euthanasia Department,* comprised a large box of diamorphine tablets, 56 pills. I took two and silently thanked my nurse-saviour.

The second box was much smaller with a red sticker on it marked *For Emergency Use Only*. Inside, there were two white capsules in a blister pack. In disbelief, I read the name of the drug. I thought about the nurse's anxious face as she pushed the bag of medication into my hand. And suddenly I understood. One pill for her and one for a loved one. Her secret stash, her defence in case the worst happened.

After an hour of rest, I felt much better. I was beginning to think that the whole day had been a bad dream. One that I could now forget with the help of the nice medication. I didn't want to revisit those dark thoughts and needless worries I'd had earlier. I would have a light supper, then a good night's sleep. In the morning, everything would look brighter.

At ten o'clock, I heard the doorbell sound. I glanced up at the viewscreen by the front door. Two androids stood on my doorstep, armed to their nasty metal teeth, their drones hovering behind them. A black van with darkened windows waited at the kerb.

There was no time for hesitation. With my good hand I popped out one of the white capsules. It was an emergency. That much was clear. I had no intention of finding out what the authorities had in store for me. As I washed the tablet down with my final gulp of tea, I only wished my lovely nurse had saved the other pill for herself.

A Roar of the Engine, a Puff of Smoke
Christopher J Wright

King William V Industrial Estate, Towcester, July 2050

Leaning over the bonnet, Jake took hold of the breaker bar and pulled slow and steady, turning the engine over. He felt an increasing resistance flowing through his wrists and arms as one of the cylinders reached full compression, then the release before it grew once more. He adjusted the breaker and pulled again. The cycle was smooth, steady, like a heartbeat.

Outside the half-opened garage door, he heard the soulless whine of an electric car driving past. In comparison, the machine before him, an old 2027 Aston Martin DB12, was a living being.

Satisfied that all was well with the engine, he reattached the auxiliary drive belt and closed the bonnet. Climbing into the driver's seat, Jake checked the drive was in neutral, depressed the brake pedal and touched the start button. The engine roared into life, settling into a satisfying growl.

With a smile, Jake closed his eyes and leaned his foot on the accelerator, hearing the familiar rise in pitch of the engine as the revs mounted. The smell of exhaust fumes drifted into the cabin. Most would wrinkle their noses at the acrid scent of imperfect combustion. To Jake, it was raw nostalgia, a reminder of better, exciting days.

Opening his eyes, Jake saw a figure at the doorway.

His watch showed four o'clock. Where had the afternoon gone?

Jake switched the engine off and climbed out of his DB12, aging muscles finding the low set of the cabin tougher than they once had.

"Mr Davis," Jake said. "Apologies for keeping you waiting."

"Not a problem." Davis grinned. "That's quite a car you've got there. Must have cost you the earth?"

"She didn't come cheap, that's for sure. When the Restriction Act kicked in, the bottom dropped out of the market for a bit. A contact at Aston Martin helped me snag her for a price I could almost afford."

Davis's eyes roamed over the sleek lines of the bodywork. "She must be a beauty to drive. Still got that contact?"

"Sorry. I was part of the pit crew for the Formula 1 team until it swapped to electric in '43. The people I knew are long gone. Aston want to forget about these old combustion models. As much as they can, anyway."

"Probably out of my league, anyhow. Is my car ready?"

Jake picked up his tablet from the service desk, pulling the invoice on to the screen. "You just needed some new spark plugs and fresh brake pads. So, full service, parts and labour, MOT and combustion engine license comes in at €2,130."

"Ouch. We don't hold on to these old girls because they're economic, do we? And all for five hundred miles a year."

"Speaking of which," Jake said. "I've got your mileage certificate for the year. 497 miles. Well judged."

"I thought about going round the block again to use another couple, but I didn't have the nerve to risk a fine."

Jake sent the payment request over to Davis's tablet, who confirmed. "Thanks, and here are your documents." He swiped them across and handed the BMW fob over.

"Are you watching the Grand Prix this weekend?" Davis said.

"Normally, I don't. It's a shell of what it used to be. But it's the hundredth anniversary this year. A few of us dinosaurs from the old days are going to meet up there."

"Hope you enjoy it. See you next year."

Jake tidied up his desk and prepared to lock up.

He heard the BMW Series 5 fire up and idle for a few moments. It came into view as it pulled away and joined the road. A roar of the engine, a puff of smoke from the exhaust and the car accelerated off out of sight, drawing a turn of heads from the workers in the unit opposite.

Jake smiled. You had to make the most of that mileage allowance.

Silverstone Circuit, Sunday 10th July

Jake stepped off the shuttle bus and looked towards the Silverstone circuit.

It was a bright, sunny morning, a handful of clouds scattered across an otherwise blue sky. The cool of the morning lingered but it promised to be a scorching summer day. Perfect for getting tyres in the zone, comfortable for cars but a nightmare for drivers. Or rather, it would be if there were any drivers.

The circuit hadn't changed much in the seven years since he'd been a part of the furniture. The temporary scaffolding stands were still visible off to the right by Club Corner. Permanent stands had been built along the Hamilton Straight but new building was on hold while F1 wrestled with its identity due to falling viewing figures and nervous sponsors.

Jake joined one of several queues at the entrance. Progress was swift and, when his turn arrived, it took only a few seconds to present his ID card. Somewhere in the ether, an AI agent confirmed that his facial scan matched the card and that he had a valid pass for race day. A green light glowed and he was waved through.

Leaving the entrance hall, Jake took a moment to get his bearings. The Abbey and Hamilton Stands towered before him. Over to the left, he picked out the Lando Norris Bar. It was still early, around ten o'clock, but the place was already filling up.

Jake slowed at the entrance, searching the tables for his old pit crew buddies.

A waving hand caught his attention. It was Greg McInlay, or Hamish, as he'd been known as soon as the crew heard his accent and saw his ruddy hair and beard. The fact that he hailed from Corby, rather than Scotland, never got in the way.

"Hamish," Jake said. "How are you?"

"Good, laddie." Hamish fell straight back into playing to the gallery. "Been a while since I went by that name."

After an awkward pause, they pulled together for a hug.

"It's good to see you," Jake said. "Let me get a look at you."

Hamish was wearing dark cargo trousers and an Aston Martin polo shirt. The uncomfortable stretch and faded look suggested it was from the old days. His ginger hair and beard were flecked with grey and there were a few more lines around the eyes.

"You look like shit, mate," Jake said with a smile. "What you having?"

"A pint of IPA. And you're looking pretty rough

yourself, Jake. Pot, meet kettle."

Jake ordered two IPAs at the bar, paying twice what they were worth. It was going to be an expensive day.

They sat at the table, swapping stories of the old days, about pranks they'd pulled on each other, the highs when the team had put drivers on the podium, the lows when the cars had fallen in Q1 despite all their hard work.

Members of the old crew arrived in ones and twos. Not everyone was there, by any means, but familiar faces, food and a steady flow of beer oiled the occasion. The group finally numbered eight, a hub of talk and laughter within the bar.

With an hour to the race, they made their way up the Abbey Stand where they had a row of seats. On the way, Hamish put a hand on Jake's shoulder, inviting him to drop back from the others.

"What's up?"

Hamish checked nobody was close by. "You've got a DB12, I'd heard."

"Yeah, she's a beauty."

"I'm betting you've never driven her. I mean, really driven her."

"Well, of course not."

"What if there was a way you could?"

"I'm listening."

"There's a marshal working here. Used to be on the Mercedes crew. He's coming up for retirement in a few weeks, and next Monday – "

"What? You're talking about breaking in to the circuit?"

"It's hardly breaking in if an official waves us through, is it?"

"I don't know. There'd be hell to pay, surely."

"There might be," Hamish nodded. "But, for a day, you'd be truly living again. Not this undeath of tinkering with engines, told we can only drive them for ten miles a week."

Jake thought back to the afternoon in the garage, losing himself in the work on the engine, the sounds and the smells of exhaust fumes and engine grease. It was precious. It meant something.

"You're a bloody fool, Hamish. I wish you well but count me out."

He looked at Jake, eyes sizing him up. "It's your loss, laddie, but I understand."

They continued on in silence, the camaraderie of the last few hours, for now, broken.

As Jake emerged from the stairwell, the view was breathtaking. A swathe of seated spectators fell away before him. The Hamilton Straight stretched from Club Corner far to the right, past the grandstand to Abbey off to the left. They'd get an excellent view of the drama leading into the first corners of the race.

Across the track, Jake saw the paddock. Pit crews attending to engines, adjusting suspensions, putting tyres into blankets. Hanging down from the roof of the stand, a screen showed the build-up to the race.

Andrea Zhang, Ferrari's lead AI developer, was

being interviewed about the latest update to their two AI Racing Drivers, or AIRDs. She hoped the improved decision-making would give them the edge over the McLaren team.

Jake followed Hamish down a few rows to their seats. They were plusher than he'd expected and each had a virtual reality headset slotted into a cradle beneath. Jake scanned his ID card and the headset was released.

They were all the rage, allowing spectators to have an immersive experience through strategically positioned cameras. For F1, that meant live feeds from the two ocular cameras on whichever AIRD was selected. "Almost like driving the car yourself" was the sales pitch. As if a glorified video game output could ever substitute for the real thing.

Jake donned his headset. The interview with Zhang was still in progress.

" – do have their own individual personalities. Although they take the same training input and all get the benefit of the same race experiences, there are noticeable differences. Max, for instance, is quite adventurous compared to Alain, who'll bide his time and wait for opportunities. In recent comparisons – "

Jake took the headset off. The AI debate wasn't one that interested him. It was just another way that the world had shifted away from gritty, messy reality. Sure, AIRDs had their personalities, but they were all variations on a theme. You didn't get the intense interactions, the dislikes, the rivalries that human drivers brought. And teams didn't have to pay their AIRDs a huge salary.

It was experimentation at first, computer geeks wondering if AIs could challenge humans. The machines had improved surprisingly quickly and there was a push by the teams to allow AIRDs into F1. Health and Safety had been the final justification. A rookie driver had died in a crash at Spa in the 2044 season. It was the first death for nearly thirty years, but it was used to drive an agenda.

The season of 2046 was the first without real people in the cockpits. Lap times were down. The AIs didn't have to worry about the G-forces like a human did. But, for Jake, it broke the magic. This was the first grand prix he'd been to since.

Three o'clock loomed.

Jake watched the pit crews in each of the bays fit the tyres to the cars, then put the tyre blankets back on to maintain the perfect temperature. In the Aston Martin bays, he saw the team's two AIRDs climb into their cockpits. The cars were still fully humanly driveable, with AIRDs required to handle the controls in the same way human drivers had. The AIRDs' mechanical nature was on show, angular metal parts on display.

It had long been recognised that trying to make robots look too real was a mistake. It left people with an eerie sense of wrongness. Even so, the use of AIRDs to replace human drivers was a mis-step. Moves were already underway to allow the teams to build the AIs directly into the car. That would save more money, of course.

The cars began to leave their garages and form up in the pit lane in qualifying order, the two McLarens at the front, followed by the Ferrari and GoogleAI cars taking the next four spots between them.

The Astons had qualified ninth and fourteenth, a middling performance for them. Once all eighteen cars had lined up, the pit lane light turned green and the cars moved off to start the formation lap.

The familiar whine of the electric motors, somewhere between an underground train and a jet engine, carried across the track as the cars accelerated. They slowed for Village before disappearing out of sight onto the Wellington Straight. A few minutes later, the cars came into sight at Club Corner, weaving to left and right along the straight to keep the tyres at temperature, before stopping in their assigned positions on the grid.

Now that they were stopped, the cars made almost no sound, just fans that could barely be heard above the noise of the spectators. The quiet was disconcerting. Engines should be idling, a murmur of contained power, waiting for the moment of release. The first red light on the gantry above the finish line shone out followed by the remaining four, one per second.

Jake tensed as the five lights held for one second, then another.

Then all the lights went out, the calm overtaken by

noise and chaos. Eighteen cars pulled away, each making a crack sound as full torque was applied. The whine of the engines rose in pitch, now loud. The cars jostled for position, one of the Ferraris passing a McLaren as the cars took the Abbey Corner. An Aston gained a couple of places, moving up to seventh.

As the field disappeared out of sight, most of the spectators around Jake put on their headsets.

Jake followed suit and was presented with options to see the race from various angles and from the perspective of any of the drivers. He followed menus to select the lead Aston Martin car and was rewarded with a view from its cockpit.

The car was rounding the slower Brooklands and Luffield turns, hard on the heels of one of the GoogleAI cars. It lost a little ground as it accelerated, closing again at the next turn. When it reached the Hangar Straight, the two cars swiftly moved to top speed, the Aston gradually closing, moving wide to try to pass.

The GoogleAI car held the racing line, holding off on the brakes for a fraction of a second longer than the Aston, to keep it at bay. Still close, the Aston followed the GoogleAI car through Vale and Club and on to the straight to complete the first lap.

From the perspective of the Aston AIRD, Jake saw the stand where he was sitting scream past. The experience in the headset had been exhilarating but, he realised, he could have experienced it just as well at home.

He took the headset off and looked around at the crowd. Almost all were engrossed in their headset experience. Few were looking directly at the cars as they sped along the straight in front of them.

Jake noticed Hamish was staring at him.

"This isn't right," Jake said, shaking his head. "That thing next week. Where do I need to be and when?"

Hamish grinned. "Never doubted you for a minute, laddie. 5:30am a week on Monday. I'll message you the location."

Jake watched the rest of the race without the headset, his mind elsewhere.

Alain Ferrari won.

Silverstone Circuit, Monday 18th July

The air was cool and the morning already bright when Jake pulled into a car park in one of the industrial units adjacent to the circuit. As he drew up, he saw the grandest selection of combustion engine cars he'd seen since leaving the Aston pit crew.

Jake identified a Porsche 911 S, a BMW M8 and a Jaguar F-Type. But his attention lingered on a papaya orange McLaren P1, one of the holy trinity of the old supercars, a vision of aerodynamic perfection.

Hamish leaned against the Jaguar, speaking with the other three drivers.

Jake got out of his DB12, glancing around to see if

they'd attracted any unwanted attention. It was quiet, no sign of anybody but the five of them.

His watch showed 5:27am. Butterflies danced in his stomach.

The roar of an approaching engine broke the morning quiet. A red Ferrari Roma rolled into the car park. Once the driver joined the others, Hamish gave his instructions.

"There's a marshal waiting to let us in. We'll join the circuit at the Loop, then form up on the F1 grid. We do five racing laps, then leave again at the Loop. Anything more than that and the risk of being stopped grows quickly. Grid position will be decided by lots."

Hamish held up six envelopes. Each driver picked one. Jake opened his to reveal a four.

"I know the blood will be pumping," Hamish said, "but, please, no contact. We all want to get home quickly and in one piece. Now, follow me and good luck."

The drivers murmured their assent and nodded to each other. Each were faces Jake recognised from pit crews in the old days. The guy driving the P1 looked especially familiar, one of the higher ups at McLaren. He must have been, to drive a car like that.

The roar as six treasured engines powered on was truly amazing, stirring something deep inside Jake. Hamish's Jaguar led the procession of cars out, over a roundabout and into the circuit complex. After a few twists and turns, they reached a part of the mesh fence with a gate. A grey-haired man wearing orange overalls with a black trim waited and pulled the gate open. Jake and the others glided through, following Hamish along a service road before weaving through a safety barrier on to the track.

The Porsche ahead of him opened up the throttle and accelerated away down the Wellington Straight.

Jake pushed hard on the accelerator. The DB12 responded immediately, shifting through the gears, pressing him into the bucket seat. He knew the track by heart from watching countless laps from the Paddock. But this was different. This was real. With a flick of his thumb, Jake switched the DB12 into Sport+ mode. He was rewarded with a surge of revs and speed and the steering felt tighter as, heart racing, he took the next corner.

At the end of the lap, he slowed to take his place on the grid. The McLaren was to his right. The Ferrari and Hamish's Jaguar were ahead, the BMW and Porsche behind.

The marshal leaned over the pit wall and raised a faded Union Jack flag high. Jake revved his engine, hearing the response of the cars around him. Focused on the flag and the Ferrari ahead, he waited.

The flag dropped.

Jake pushed the accelerator to the floor. The wheels spun for a moment, then gripped and thrust the car forward, gears shifting upwards rapidly. He reached 60mph before even taking a breath. Even so, the Ferrari surged ahead, the Porsche drew level, while the McLaren had breezed past Hamish and was already leading the group. When they reached Abbey, Jake was just behind Hamish. The Porsche was on his outside, though still behind.

The Porsche pushed Jake wide at the next turn, overtaking and slotting in behind Hamish. Jake ran fifth with only the BMW behind.

But the DB12 was in its element, surging along the straights, hugging the racing line on the corners and hounding Hamish's Jaguar all through the turns leading up to the Hangar Straight. Jake floored the accelerator, using the DB12's animal power to surge past the Jaguar under braking into Stowe, then maintained position through Vale and Club to finish the first lap.

Jake focused on the track, holding the line, using all the power he could, braking as late as he dared. The second and third laps passed. Hamish dropped slowly back and up ahead Jake could see the red of the Ferrari Roma drawing closer.

By the end of the fourth lap, he was almost in range of the Ferrari, bearing in through the early turns of the circuit. On the Wellington Straight, he used the slipstream to draw closer. Too close, a voice murmured in his head. Through Maggotts, the steering wobbled in the dirty air behind the Roma. Jake corrected but lost ground. On the Hangar Straight, it was all he could do to get back in range again.

He hounded the Ferrari through Stowe,

slingshotting out of Club as the finish approached. The nose of the DB12 edged along the body of the Roma, but the finish line came too soon. He was still behind but close enough to see relief on his rival's face.

The marshal waved the chequered flag as the two cars screamed through.

As Jake eased off the accelerator, the engine settled down from a roar to a growl and, finally, a soft purr. The beast within was tamed once more. Hands trembling, Jake slumped back into his seat, his adrenaline completely drained.

At the Loop, the two cars parked next to the McLaren and Porsche were already waiting. Jake climbed out of the DB12 and approached the Ferrari. The driver met him, a huge grin on his face.

"Hell of a race, mate," Jake said, holding out his hand.

They shook hands and, before Jake knew it, they were locked in an embrace.

Hamish's Jaguar and the BMW soon arrived.

Shortly after, the marshal joined them in his own car.

"We'd better get out of here, now," Hamish called out. "Remember this day."

As the procession made its way along the service road and out of the circuit, Jake half-expected flashing blue lights and a roadblock. But there was nothing.

There would be consequences, no doubt. It was hard to see how this could go unnoticed.

But whatever happened, Hamish had been right.

Jake was buzzing. He'd lived in a way he thought would never happen again.

In the Beyond

Introducing Master Ajax Ambrose

Allan Shipham

"Grandpa Jack!" said a fair-haired, freckled girl in dungarees. "Can you tell us another story about the old days in Wellingborough when you were a boy?"

Both grandchildren stopped colouring in and looked up.

Grandpa Jack looked around the room. "There is one man," he said, "I don't talk about much. He showed up in Wellingborough, was here for a few hours and we never saw him again. Would you like to hear about him?"

The children set down their colouring pencils and sat on the two-seater sofa in front of the old man. Siblings often bicker but Colin and Pollyanna sat close to each other so they could hold hands if they got scared. Pollyanna reassured her little brother with a comforting hug and she braced herself.

"I remember it, as if it were yesterday," Grandpa Jack reminisced, he liked telling stories. "I was a boy, the world was less confused and everyone had something to do. I was a bit older than you and life was a lot simpler.

"My mum worked as a district nurse and spent a lot of time on her bicycle going village to village, house to house at all hours. We made our own fun. In the summer, me, Ralph and Peter would go down to the Nene at Ditchford and swim all morning. There was a signal hut there and the guard used to keep a goat. If we had a few pennies, we'd club together and buy a bottle of goat's milk. Oh, I can remember the taste today. Then we'd swim upstream to London Road Station. We didn't come home until we were hungry."

The old man gazed into the empty fireplace for a few moments and settled back into his seat. "It was a hot summer day. We'd had a dry spell and everything was a bit parched and withered."

"Who's the man you don't talk about much?" Colin said.

"Is he a ghost?" Pollyanna said.

"I'm getting there!" Grandpa said, smiling at the girl.

"The train from Northampton pulled into London Road Station. We had two stations in them days. It was a normal steam train but we always liked to watch who got off and guess what their business was in the town.

"A strange young man hopped along the tracks following the train. His behaviour was very odd, jumping around like a grasshopper. He wore clothes we'd never seen before, and when I was close to him, he smelled of something unusual, not sulphur but very similar. His waistcoat, jacket and trousers shimmered like mercury in the sun. He saw us from the railway line and called us over."

"Couldn't he afford a ticket for the train?"

"I don't know, I never asked," Jack chuckled. "He seemed a bit lost. He asked us what date it was.

"'Tuesday!' I said.

"'No! What year?'

"'It's 1932,' I added, a little confused. 'The first week of June'.

"Mouse and Ginger sniggered. They thought he'd escaped from the asylum in Northampton.

"'Great! I'm not late!' he said, shaking our hands. 'I'm Master Ajax Ambrose, nice to meet you!'

"'Master?' I said.

"Master Ambrose frowned like I was speaking a foreign language.

"'Late for what?' I asked.

"That's when things got a bit weird. He stared at me like we were related and asked if my name was Jack! You could have knocked me down with a feather. How did he know my name?"

"Did he hear your friends call you Jack?"

"I thought that, Pollyanna, but then I remembered we had nicknames for each other back then. Mine was 'Winkle', Ralph was 'Mouse' and Peter was 'Ginger'."

They giggled.

"How did he know your name?" Colin said. "Mum says never talk to strangers!"

"Mum's right, but, like I said, these were different

times. Strangers were just friends you hadn't made yet."

"What did you tell him?" Pollyanna said.

"I told him yes," Jack smiled. "My mum always said tell the truth.

"He knelt down and spoke to me. He said he'd travelled a long way and had an important message for me. I was so shocked. Someone I didn't know had travelled a long way with a message for me!"

"What was the message?" The children were enthralled.

"He told me that soon I had to trust someone, a stranger I had no reason to trust, that he was a good man and that the future depended on it!"

"What does that mean, Grandpa?"

"I would find out later, but I was shocked into silence. I was uncomfortable and still a bit confused." He shook his head.

"Master Ambrose then asked us where Wellingborough was. If he'd turned around he'd have seen the sign."

"Maybe he couldn't read?" Pollyanna suggested.

Their grandpa paused and shook his head. "Now you come to mention it, maybe he couldn't. I never thought of that!" He reached to his waistcoat pocket and cupped something through the material. "You know… he wanted me, Mouse and Ginger to show him the way to town," he said, nodding. "I know that now.

"Well, Master Ambrose seemed to be in a bit of a

rush. He said he needed to be at St Luke's Church and it was very important. We were confused at first, because there wasn't a St Luke's. But, then I remembered overhearing some workmen talking about St Luke's when they were working in All Hallows. I didn't understand, but later learned the church was called St Luke's in the past. Anyway, we offered to show him the way, as we were heading back home.

"As we walked to Wellingborough together, Master Ambrose told us some very interesting stories. He said he travelled to some unusual places and knew some interesting people. I thought his stories were fanciful, superheroes and aliens, but then I saw some of his stories in comics when I was older. If I had written down his stories and sold them, I'd be a rich man!"

"Why did he need to be at St Luke's?" Colin said, engrossed in the old man's story.

"Why did they change the name of the church?" Pollyanna said.

"Church Street," Jack said, shrugging his shoulders, "around the back of All Hallows was being dug up. The road was very narrow and they wanted to make it wider for horse carts, automobiles and lorries. Sadly, they had to dig up some old graves in the graveyard and move them. It's weird to think of those people laying in peace for all that time and then being dug up to make the road wider. You know, there were Anglo-Saxon graves, some of the oldest in

Wellingborough.

"There were a lot of visitors wearing suits who came to take a look and they had public meetings about it and there were articles in the newspapers. Our parents didn't want us hanging around the graveyard while the work was carried out. They said it was disrespectful. But curiosity got the better of us and we found a way to get a good view of what was going on."

"Did you climb up the trees?"

"And roof tops,' Jack said. "But the grown-ups didn't see us and our parents didn't find out."

The old man smiled again, remembering lost friends and fond memories.

"We took Master Ambrose to All Hallows like he'd asked and he spoke with the Clerk of Works who was in charge of all the work. He was a short man with black, round glasses and a bowler hat. He was bossy and kept telling people to clear off, except when the vicar came out to check on the progress. Oh, he was nice then.

"We didn't want to be seen, so we were on the roof tops looking down. Things got a bit heated with Master Ambrose and they ended up shouting at each other. It was entertaining for us to see grown-ups falling out and we could hear what they were saying.

"Master Ambrose was furious they were digging up the bodies and protested several times. He kept pulling out a curious, gold pocket watch on a chain from his pocket and checking the time. The watch was very old, maybe ancient. It had small blue stones mounted on both sides of the case. I'd not seen one like it before. He pressed small buttons on the side of the watch and put it back in his waistcoat.

"Then he was shouting at the Clerk of Works again. The workmen would stop and the Clerk would get them working again. At one point, Master Ambrose pulled a shovel away from one of the workers and there was a tug o' war to get it back.

"We thought it was funny," Jack chuckled, "but Master Ambrose was very angry. All the time, his suit glistened in the afternoon sun. It was quite a sight."

"What happened to all the Angli-Saxons?"

"Anglo-Saxons? Oh, they're laid to rest at the cemetery on London Road. They also dug up a graveyard on Outlaw Lane at the same time. They all rest in new graves. They were strange times for the town. You think when you're laid to rest, they'll leave you alone. You know, they say all good things come to an end. I suppose that goes for graves as well.

"Anyway, then there was a loud crunch. One of the workers who were digging the graves had hit the lid of a coffin. It was weird because they hadn't dug up many wooden coffins. They must have rotted away with time or the people might not have been buried in wood. Unlucky for the grave digger, his spade broke the lid while Master Ambrose was watching.

"Master Ambrose became even more furious. It was strange because he was polite to us and then turned angry with the people disturbing the graves. Most of the remains were put into new coffins to be moved."

The children were uncomfortable hearing about coffins and graves. Holding each other's hands, they listened intently.

"The sky turned black, thunder rang out and lightning lit the darkness. We were only swimming in the sun an hour before, now it was stormy and tempestuous. It reminded me of Sunday School when we were told the sky went black on Good Friday, the heavens opened and it started to rain. I borrowed a tarpaulin from the dairy yard. We hid under it and clung to the ridge of the roof, so we could watch what happened. I don't think the weather had anything to do with disturbing the graves but it did make me wonder for years after."

Jack's face became pale and gaunt. The children shuffled forward on their seat so they didn't miss anything.

"The lid came away in a couple of pieces and the gravediggers threw them to one side. One of the diggers had to jump down into the grave and pass the ropes carefully under what was left of the coffin. The workmen lit oil lamps in the drizzle so they could see better. They must've expected it to go on all night. The ground was hard to dig when it was wet, which made it difficult.

"First, we noticed the corpse was wasted away down to brilliant white bone. It always surprises me when I see a skeleton. Then we saw the dead man's jacket, waist coat and trousers shimmering in the lamp light. It was the same shimmer that Master Ambrose's clothes made."

Jack lifted his finger. "Even the workmen were surprised."

He settled back in his seat.

"As they lifted the coffin at the feet end, a pocket watch slid out of the waistcoat and hit the skeleton's jaw. It was exactly the same kind of gold watch that Master Ambrose had. It even had the little blue stones.

"The Clerk of Works kept telling Master Ambrose to keep a few steps away from the workmen. He was also stunned into silence when he saw the clothes on the corpse and especially when he caught sight of the watch.

"'What's going on here?' the Clerk of Works growled.

"The workmen stepped back away from the grave in fear and confusion.

"'You're messing with things you don't understand,' Master Ambrose warned. 'Give me that watch and I'll be on my way!'

"I was glued to the spot. We'd never seen anything like it. Mouse and Ginger said we should get out of there. I think the thunderstorm unnerved them even more than the bodies. I said we should stay and see what happened. They left. I don't think they wanted to get wet again.

"'Grave goods will be re-buried with the owners,' said the Clerk of Works. 'This is none of your business. I'll summon a police officer if you don't clear off!'

"There were more heated words.

"I wanted to catch up with my friends but something kept me back.

"Scanning the trees and rooftops, Master Ambrose caught sight of me. There was a moment when I thought he was going to tell everyone I was watching. Instead, he did something quite odd. He took out his watch, checked the time again and went across the graveyard to a grave that had an angel and some flowers. He knelt down, out of sight of the workmen and the Clerk of Works and discreetly placed something on the ground. He looked up again to see if I noticed, winked and went back to the graveside again. He stalked the open grave like a fox ready to pounce when the others weren't looking.

"I couldn't leave. The whole thing was getting so mysterious.

"The workmen prepared the larger coffin and were getting ready to put the corpse in its new home. Master Ambrose raced towards it and grabbed the corpse's watch. There was a struggle with a workman. Master Ambrose pressed some buttons on the older watch and then there was a hot, brilliant, white light.

"I couldn't see what was happening.

"A wave of energy pushed the workmen to the ground. It knocked down the tools leaning against the wall. I lost my footing and slipped down the roof. My hair stood up on the back of my neck. I was trembling."

Gasping, Pollyanna stood up.

"Strange thing. The clouds cleared and the sun came out again. Just like that!"

Jack rubbed his chin in deep thought. "I scrambled back to the ridge and peered over the edge. Something very peculiar had happened. Master Ambrose had disappeared in the bright light. The workman and Clerk got to their feet and brushed themselves down.

"'What happened?' one of the men said.

"'I don't know,' the Clerk said.

Pollyanna sat down again and gripped her brother's hand.

"'My memory's blank,' one workman said. 'I can't remember anything, since we arrived this morning.'

"They looked at the open grave.

"''Ere, we must've dug this guy up in the shiny suit. I think we were about to put him in this coffin.'

"I didn't hang around. I scrambled down the roof, shimmied down the drainpipe and raced home. I never spoke a word of what I saw. Not to anyone. As far as I know, I'm the only one who remembers anything about it."

"Did you never see Master Ambrose again?" Pollyanna said.

"No," Jack said. "But later that day, I went back to the graveyard. I wanted to know what was left by the angel. The workmen had finished and there was no-one around. The open grave had been backfilled and there were a couple of red squirrels foraging in the cool evening air.

"I sneaked over to the grave with an angel where Master Ambrose had dropped something. I found something shiny beside the flowers.

"Just then, I was disturbed by an old stranger in a long, dark-grey coat that reached to the ground. His coat had a large hood. In the diminishing light, I could barely see the man's eyes, let alone his face. There was something familiar about his voice, but it was old and I couldn't place it."

Jack could see the children were scared.

"It was okay, it was all okay!

"The man said 'Jack, don't be frightened! You don't know me but I've always looked out for you and will do so in the future. Don't be scared by what you saw today.' I remembered what Master Ambrose had said about trusting a stranger. How did he know? He placed a hand on my shoulder to reassure me.

"'In fact,' he said, 'you're probably likely to see much weirder things and have strange adventures of your own. What you have there is a weapon for good or a weapon for evil. It's for you to make the right choices and pass it on when the time is right. Keep it safe and keep it from people who'd do harm.'

"Then, as fast as he appeared, he was gone."

The door to the kitchen opened and a woman emerged with a metal tray. On the tray were two cups of tea, two beakers of orange squash and some custard creams on a plate.

"I hope you haven't been filling their minds with ghost stories again, Dad!"

"Where is Master Ambrose now?" Colin said.

"Who's Master Ambrose?" Mum said.

Grandpa smiled again.

"Er, I went back the next day and found the coffin lid pieces. One had a brass plate on it with a date. May, 1592. And the name Master Ajax Ambrose. That's all I ever knew!"

There was silence as the children thought about what they'd heard.

The children took a couple of custard creams each and got on with eating them.

"You know," Jack said, "all those other graves were much older. That coffin had no business being there!"

"Could he be a time traveller," Pollyanna said, "like Doctor Who?"

"Coffins!" Mum said, shaking her head. "Doctor Who?"

"Maybe he was a time traveller?" Colin said.

Jack reached into his pocket and took out a watch on a chain. He opened the case and looked at the time. Several blue gemstones glistened in the light against the gold case. The children hadn't seen it before. They gasped as Jack put it back in his pocket.

"I've always been confused," Jack whispered, "by complex, space-time continuum paradoxes."

Roses around the Door

Pat Aitcheson

My father told me he was obsessed with engines, even as a lad. He spent his youth tinkering with old bangers and bikes, landed an apprenticeship in automotive engineering and eventually got his dream gig working on F1 race cars. That's how we ended up living near Silverstone, in a little cottage with roses by the door, that whole country vibe.

I was away at Birmingham Uni when he turned up out of the blue. Heard a knock and, when I opened my door, there he was, standing a couple of steps back wearing his usual lopsided grin and green and black leathers.

"Hey, sweetheart."

"Dad? What are you doing here? Not that I don't want to see you but – "

"You're okay," he said softly. "You're going to be okay, both of you." He grimaced, left hand pressed to his neck. "I can't – I wanted – sorry love – "

"Dad, what – "

He swayed and, as I darted forward, went pale. Before I could catch him, he simply faded away, lips parted and gaze unfocused. My arms closed around empty air and my mouth opened on a scream that brought my housemates running.

Later, Gemma would tell me I kept repeating, "He's gone," over and over, even before my mum's anguished phone call, and that my hands felt so icy cold she gave me gloves and a hand warmer.

The M1 around Wakefield is notorious for accidents. Even an experienced biker like my dad stood no chance against a car full of drunk football fans. One wet Wednesday in March as night was falling, my world tilted and went dark.

In the aftermath, Mum and I clung to each other, shivering in the bed they once shared, both of us hollowed out by silent grief.

"Do you believe in life after death?" Even my whisper seemed to echo in the quiet.

"I wish I did," Mum said bitterly. "I wanted him to sell that bloody bike but, no, he promised to be careful. But there's always the other guy and I – "

She gripped my arms tight enough to bruise and broke down into sobbing again. Her quiet despair cut so much deeper than wailing ever could.

That's how she was when we went together to identify him, staring at his face that looked so peaceful, unlike the horror concealed under the sheets. She shook and gasped and would have collapsed if the kind man with us hadn't been ready to support her.

I could never tell her my dad had somehow sent

one last message, his soul reaching out at exactly 19.27 as the sun vanished. Why me and not her? I had no answer, no explanation and nothing to offer that would ease her pain. Mum left our picturesque cottage behind and moved back to York to be near her sister. I stayed around Birmingham after graduation for work. I had good friends, was happily single and mostly enjoyed my work in Human Resources.

There had been odd happenings over the years, even before a promotion brought me back to my home county. Hair standing up on end and sudden cold patches of air were plausibly explained by sitting in a draught or coming down with a cold. Occasionally, a doorway filled me with unformed dread and I had to force myself to go through. I was working long hours, eating irregularly, stressed out by deadlines and needed a holiday.

I had my vision checked after seeing a man in a waistcoat and old-fashioned breeches walk across a crowded pub bar before vanishing through the wall. That would have been noteworthy enough, but when you added in the fact that he was floating above our heads and nobody else seemed to have seen him, it was clear something wasn't adding up.

After developing tinnitus, I got my hearing checked. The doctor said it was probably temporary after an inner ear virus infection. Reassured that my hearing was normal, I listened to music through wireless headphones until I learned to tune it out.

Despite that, only a month later, I found myself turning to look for crying children on a stately home tour. Perhaps it was a group in the next room, though why would anyone drag children to see things they couldn't appreciate escaped me.

A visit to the basement of my friend's newly renovated village home was the tipping point.

"Rose. I was just saying we had to excavate the floor to get more headroom. Are you even listening?"

Confused, I turned to Mel. "Did you get a dog? I hear barking."

Smiling, Mel rolled her eyes. "You're really not with it today. You've been kinda jumpy and now this. Oh, I bet it's low blood sugar. Let's get you some tea and cake. I finally got a boiling water tap and it's so convenient. You should get one."

She led the way back upstairs chatting about brownies and steam ovens while the dog's bark faded away, echoing oddly. True, I had been sleeping badly but the tinnitus was less intrusive than before. Still, it was unnerving.

Strange experiences had become woven into my life, even though I never saw my dad again, in dreams or real life. I decided to search out supposedly haunted locations to prove I was mistaken, my body was playing tricks on me and I was no more tuned in to spirit radio than the next twentysomething woman.

Armed with internet searches, I compiled a list of places to visit in my free time. The old St Crispin's Mental Hospital stood roofless and abandoned after a fire, its clock tower keeping vigil as if daring the modern houses built around it to come closer. All I sensed was the usual melancholy of abandoned buildings, shot through with the knowledge of the misery endured by asylum inmates in previous centuries.

I visited the World's End at Ecton on Hallowe'en, but despite hunkering down in my car wrapped in a blanket with everything switched off, there was no sign of the grey-robed nun with a skull for a face.

The Hind Hotel in Wellingborough served a good meal in the restaurant, with no trace of a crying girl or any of Cromwell's forces on their way to crushing the Royalists at Naseby.

One by one, I ticked off my list until one remained.

The days shrank as the solstice approached but, despite that, my mood remained buoyant. My self-imposed quest was almost at an end and then it would be time to celebrate my birthday and a quiet Christmas with Mum and my aunt's family. Maybe I'd even see a cousin or two.

The afternoon of December 21st found me picking my way between headstones whose inscriptions were lost to time and creeping moss. I cursed, trying not to slip on the wet grass leading downhill. Like so many others, St John the Baptist's Church in Boughton was likely built over an earlier pagan place of worship. This site incorporated a sacred spring, now found under the east wall.

The sound of water led me on, my breath clouding in the cool air. In this faded light, the tumbled walls appeared grey, leached of the warm sandstone hues displayed in online photos.

"Is that it?" I muttered, decidedly underwhelmed by the light trickle of water emerging from a little stone culvert. I poked at it with my boot then pulled out my phone to check the time.

"It's more impressive before Midsummer."

A soft voice startled me, my phone slipping from my numb fingers. I whirled around to find a woman standing nearby, her red hair a splash of colour in the gloom.

"Sorry, what?"

How had she crept up on me?

I picked up my phone and wiped it on my jeans' leg with a shaky hand.

"The water," she said. "It ebbs and flows during the year but it never stops. Perhaps you heard it."

She tilted her head and regarded me with eyes of a peculiarly washed-out shade. I couldn't decide if they were green, blue or grey in the half-light.

"Easy to miss things if you aren't listening," she went on.

I backed away, already cold and feeling my gut churn. "Yeah, no, I must be going. 'Bye."

My legs moved sluggishly while my mind raced, recalling the old stories of meeting a red-haired woman who would talk with you, then ask for a kiss and another meeting in a month. Except that meeting would not take place in the land of the living. But she only appeared to men, so why had I –

"Careful now," a deeper voice said next to my ear, "or you'll fall."

I stumbled and barely stayed upright. "Get away from me!"

The light had faded. The gates seemed far away. I had to watch my feet but, when I glanced up, a tall figure loomed beyond crooked gravestones. The world was bathed in greyscale against which its shock of red hair glowed.

Still the voice spoke, too close by.

"I just want to talk."

"No, no, no – "

One last push and my hand closed around a gate latch so cold it burned my skin.

I ran for the car, flung myself in and locked the doors. Breathless and shivering, I put my head in my hands and counted shaky breaths for slow minutes until I found a tissue to wipe my tears. Eventually, I risked a glance back at the churchyard. Even the sign proclaiming it to be hallowed ground was swallowed by darkness. No red, no movement, no sound even.

"Okay. Time to go," I muttered and turned the ignition key. Music filled the car and the lights were salvation as I sang along all the way home to cover the ringing in my ears and the pulse beating a heavy rhythm in my throat. That night, St Crispin's bell tower rang and rang through my dreams.

Sunday dawned cool but clear and I dragged

myself out of bed to make tea. My Christmas gifts were wrapped and ready, so I just needed to pack a small bag before taking a leisurely drive up the M1 while it was still light.

When the knock came I dashed downstairs, happy that my last-minute delivery had arrived. Instead, I opened the door to my mother.

There were dark smudges under her eyes and she hugged herself tightly, standing a few steps away. "Rosie, darling," she whispered with a tiny smile. "Happy birthday."

Ice poured down my spine. She hadn't called me that since forever.

"Mum, no."

I reached out but she was too far away – ringing filled my ears, a thousand whispers, no words –

"You'll be fine," she said, nodding. "Listen and be safe."

She stretched fading arms towards me and I embraced nothing but coolness like sea mist on my face, falling back as my door shut with finality, with no-one to hear my scream.

The call came from my aunt an hour later. I listened to her cry, grief already lodged deep in my heart like an old enemy dug in for a siege, unwelcome yet familiar. Through her tears came a story of black ice, a narrow bridge, a deep river. Mum had no chance of survival.

"Rose, you'll come today?"

"Of course. I'm packed already."

"Be safe won't you?" she sniffled. "Please." She took a deep breath. "There's no rush."

On my way to the motorway, I made a detour which, when I thought about it, was inevitable.

A red-haired figure waited near the spring. My ears filled with the sound of rushing water much greater than the trickling spring should produce and, as the sun sank below the horizon, a single red rose in full bloom floated out of the culvert to land at my feet.

"Will you listen?"

The voice was in my ear but I felt no alarm.

"Do I have a choice?"

"Always."

It was a sigh of wind among leaves, of water running over pebbles, of the tide rushing out to the sea.

"And if I refuse?"

"Those who are not heard shout louder. Sanity lives in silence."

Voices and bells filled my ears, then quietened to a faint roar. Easily ignored. Constant.

"What is required of me?"

A change in the air, something shifting below the surface like a key sliding home. I allowed myself to be caught.

"You came into this world as the old year ended and gave way to the new. Now you are called to stand at the threshold of life for those who cannot cross. One petal, one soul, one story."

I picked up the rose with its many velvet petals

and inhaled its strong, sweet scent. Nothing should be this vital at midwinter.

I plucked a petal. "Tell me your tale and I will listen."

* * * * *

There's a red rose on my bedside table in full bloom, sitting on a plain wooden box. Each night before I go to sleep, I tug at an outer petal. It comes away easily and I place it in the box alongside all the others.

Maybe when the box is full, maybe when I pull the last petal, maybe if the rose wilts, I will be free.

Alone

Jason McClean

One

Ryan was not alone.

His eyes flickered open. He instantly registered the pale light and barely audible white noise. Like a kettle starting to warm up.

He glanced to the side of his bed. His phone screen was lit. Calling to him, he thought. It shouldn't be. He had it in DND – Do Not Disturb – he wasn't one for receiving messages when he was asleep.

It was a cool night, so he flicked his hand out of the duvet cover, grabbed his phone and quickly returned it, his hand and head below the duvet.

White noise and a blizzard on his screen.

It was only six months old and it was broken.

A pang of anger, quickly replaced by relief when he remembered it was still under warranty. He pressed and held the power button.

"Do you believe in ghosts?" The words appeared on the screen. Blizzard background and white noise still there.

Thoughts of sleep and rest vanished.

"Do you want to meet me, Ryan?"

He sat bolt upright and shoved the duvet away. He wasn't cold anymore. The phone had addressed him by name.

Well, of course it would know his name. He had named it Ryan's Phone in the settings menus when he bought it.

But he caught himself. It wasn't his phone speaking with him. It had to be someone sending a message.

"I want to meet you."

There was a presence nearby. His senses told him that without any doubt. Primal fear took over.

He grabbed his phone, bolted out of his bedroom and ran down the hallway shared with the flat upstairs. It was a safe downstairs flat on Oxford Street, Kettering. Far enough out of the town to avoid trouble. A twist of the external door handle and he ran out into the street.

Cars lined both sides of the road, electric bulbs in every other lamp post offering some light. Council savings meant there were plenty of pools of darkness but that didn't bother him.

He looked at his phone. "Who is this?" he blurted at the snowy screen.

The snow flurried. The white noise made noise.

A light came on in the house across the street, the upstairs bedroom. Curtains twitched. Eleanor's face appeared at the window. A frown wasn't far behind.

Acutely aware he was standing in the middle of the street, in the middle of the night, wearing only boxer shorts, Ryan walked to his door. It was still open. He was feeling the cold now.

He checked his phone.

There, on the screen, very clearly in plain text. "I am a ghost."

He was cold but a chill still ran down his spine. Followed quickly by a pang of anger. It had to be a prank. He whipped round and looked up and down the street.

Quiet, nightly silent, not even cars driving in nearby streets. No-one visible, apart from Eleanor, whose frown had developed into a shake of the head before turning around and closing the curtains.

When she disappeared, Ryan felt very alone. He didn't want her to leave. Maybe her watching was keeping the person, the ghost – no, the prankster – at bay.

But he didn't feel totally alone. The message was on his phone screen. He took one last look around and then stepped over the threshold and shut the door. His phone vibrated and the screen flashed back to normal, his apps on display and clock declaring 0304. He unlocked it and found the DND still in play.

While in the hallway, he checked messages and social media. Nothing unusual. Apart from the certainty he was alone again. That feeling when you walk into a house and know instinctively whether there is anyone there. Soldiers, police and even thieves swear they can tell immediately. Scientists say it's the body's electrical currents interacting with the surroundings. Your aura.

Ryan knew he was alone. And knowing that made him certain that earlier he had not been alone. The sense of someone or something else was gone. So was the snowy screen and creepy white noise.

Another thought came to him. Battery use indicator. It would tell him what app had taken control of his screen, how much battery it had used. Probably some sort of malware deep in his phone. He flicked through to the battery screen and stared.

It said his phone had been inactive up until now.

He powered the phone off and returned to bed. His head was spinning but he was also tired. He had work in the morning and needed sleep. It didn't come easily.

Two

"Sounds like your phone is haunted," Pat said, knocking a fence post into place with one massive thump from a sledgehammer. "I'll take it off your hands if you like, need a new phone."

"Shut up, I am being serious," Ryan sighed. "It wasn't a normal screen. It was all black and white snow, like old school TV interference. Then it disappeared."

"Another post."

Ryan handed him another post and Pat lined it up.

"Was it you, Pat? Did you screw around with me last night? It's the sort of thing you'd do."

Pat, hard to believe, looked a little offended and upset at the accusation, then smiled. "Wasn't me, but I wish I'd thought of it. Maybe we should do it on Dipper."

Ryan sighed again. "Dipper doesn't have a phone. He's a dinosaur."

Pat nodded and thumped another fence post into place. The work was going well, the ground damp with little bedrock to slow them down. The Boughton Estate needed a lot of fencing. It was always good well-paid work for the firm.

"Must be haunted, like I said," Pat said.

"I don't believe in ghosts. Someone has got my number. Or I've been hit with a virus."

"Maybe it was Dipper," Pat laughed.

Ryan smiled and handed him another post.

Three

Ryan reversed into a space on the road not far from his flat. It was always a nightmare parking and his car had accumulated various dents and scratches from where other vehicles had tagged him over time.

He liked Oxford Street. It sounded grand and it was his first home away from his parents. The flat was laid out over one floor, one decent-sized bedroom, kitchen, dining room and bathroom. All well-proportioned the way houses built around the

1920s had been.

Eleanor was watching from her window opposite. He smiled at her and she quickly disappeared behind her curtain. She was a funny fish. He didn't know whether it may be her dicking with his phone or he should ask her out on a date. She was pretty when she wasn't frowning. Worked as a Teaching Assistant at Tresham College.

His senses (aura) told him the flat was devoid of life. That was good until he remembered Pat's warning of it being his phone that was haunted, not the flat.

Either way, his senses told him he was alone. Time for dinner, he was starving, then it was off to the gym at the bottom of Hospital Hill for a quick workout and to see if the brunette who smiled at him last time was there. He had a story to tell her if she was.

Of course, the brunette wasn't there and, when he came home, the flat was still as devoid of life as before. He watched telly for a bit and then went to bed after an hour on his PlayStation. Living by himself gave him freedoms that he was now used to. It was also a bit lonely.

He settled into bed.

Upstairs was a bolthole for Sharon, who spent most of the week in London working. And staying over most nights shagging, no doubt. She was basically never at home, and it was no different tonight, no noisy drama upstairs.

His phone's home screen glowed at him gently,

true tone on to protect his eyes. He needed the alarm, so he set it and then put it down, wary of it, expecting the snowy screen to appear. But it didn't. Even so, he decided to switch it off at the power button. He didn't fancy anyone pranking him two nights in a row. Powered down, he left it on his bedside table and fell asleep, exhausted.

He woke up a while later, lathered in sweat, breathing hard.

The room was illuminated with a jagged white light.

His phone was on. The screen was snowy and all of Ryan's senses were on high alert. The lizard part of his brain was telling him he was not alone. It was telling him, time to fight or run. Running would be preferable, but he was in bed, and it wasn't immediately practical.

The dirty white light was casting shadows around the room. His wardrobe loomed ominously in the corner. Could someone be inside it?

His desk had dark nooks and crannies. The clothes draped over his chair were shaped like a person. He half-expected them to rise.

Hairs prickling, he scanned the room and decided there was no-one there. Then the white haze was punctuated by writhing shapes. He looked at his impossibly on, powered-up phone.

Words were appearing on screen.

He hadn't switched it on. Could someone else do that remotely? He had heard stories about phones listening in to conversations even when switched off. Talk about a Big Mac when your phone is off and then switch it on. A MacDonalds advert appears within minutes. Your phone was never really switched off.

Maybe a virus had complete control of his phone? Could switch it on when it liked.

But, deep down, that little lizard brain of his knew that wasn't true.

He wasn't alone.

"Hi, Ryan, how are you?" scrawled on to the phone screen.

Now he was shaking.

"Who is this?" he said aloud. "It's not funny you know."

"Shall we meet, Ryan? I'd really like to."

The last thing Ryan wanted was to meet whoever it was writing creepy messages. But then again, if he met them, he could knock them out for waking him up.

"Where are you?"

An enormous thud cracked down on the floor above his head.

Screaming, Ryan jumped out of bed in one bound, flight – in the first instant – easily beating fight. Then he stopped. It was his flat, damn it. Sharon might have come back from London early.

"Let's meet," flashed on his phone screen.

Another heavy thud.

Then another, heading towards the door above, towards the stairs down to the shared hallway.

They weren't thuds. They were slow footsteps – ponderous, heavy, ominous, powerful. Threatening.

Ryan grabbed his keys and sprinted out the door, leaving it wide open. He turned only when in the middle of the street, staring back, waiting for the owner of the footsteps to come down the stairs.

The flats were dark. He waited intently, focused, ready to run or fight. Who was he kidding? Run.

"You okay, Ryan?"

Yelping, he turned.

Eleanor was there in her night dress, eyes gentle and hesitant, a little scared at the same time.

Ryan was acutely aware he was wearing only boxer shorts. Again. Two nights in a row.

"Err," he managed. "Ehm."

"You'll catch your death of cold out here," she said. "Everything all right in the flat? Not a fire or something?"

The flat was pitch black and the door looked like the open maw of a huge hellhound, waiting to devour him. But it wasn't on fire. That was clear.

"You are shivering." Her frown returned.

"I thought I heard someone at my car," he blurted out, looking back at the door, seeing only inky blackness.

"Your car is down there, where you parked it," she said, pointing. "Do you want me to check it? You got the keys?"

His keys were in the door, swallowed by darkness.

Her hand touched his elbow, "Come on, let's get

you inside. Maybe a nightmare?"

She guided him towards the gaping mouth and, despite the cold night, he couldn't help but stop, breath rising, sweat spotting on his skin.

"Is there someone in there?" she whispered. "Are you being robbed?"

Robberies were common in Kettering and he would have much preferred that to what was happening to him.

"I'm okay, thanks, Eleanor." He walked towards the door, heart racing, and then stepped inside.

The thumping steps were gone.

Sharon's flat was empty.

No sign of life. His aura knew it to be true.

Eleanor appeared beside him, staring around the hallway and open door.

"You look scared," she said, frown giving way to a teasing smile. "I don't think you should be left alone."

Ryan's fear evaporated as other instincts kicked in. She really did look pretty when she wanted to. As they went to bed, he noticed his phone was powered down.

He'd worry about it in the morning.

Four

Ryan woke up lazily in the morning, no alarm sounding, only a gentle rise to consciousness. He was content.

Eleanor was looking at him, head propped up on

hand, elbow on bed. Her usual frown was replaced with a slight upturn of her lips. A shine in her eyes.

Ryan was happy. For the first time in a while. He smiled and she beamed.

"I've got to go to work soon," she said.

"Damn, same for me."

He shot up and grabbed his phone. It was off and he powered it up. Then he remembered why he had powered it down. Like a butterfly launching from a flower, his happiness took flight.

He rustled up some toast and jam and they left together. At the door, Eleanor stood on her tiptoes and kissed him on the cheek. "Will I see you later?"

"Try and stop me."

Smiling, Ryan got in his car. It would be a rush to get to Boughton Estate but if traffic was clear, he'd be fine. He chucked his phone on the passenger seat.

He made it to the fencing site off the Geddington to Grafton Road with five minutes to spare. He killed the engine and grabbed his phone.

The screen was snowing.

He gasped.

As if being typed in real time, words appeared. "Nice to meet Eleanor. Do bring her back."

Five

"You seem distracted. Everything OK?" Eleanor was serving up pasta in her little first-floor flat. It smelled great but Ryan was staring at his phone screen.

"Just thinking is all," he said. It was true. He was wondering if he was being pranked or haunted. "Haunted," he snorted with disbelief.

"What? Did you say 'haunted'?" Eleanor's frown came back.

He quite liked it now. Endearing, not hostile like it was only twenty-four hours before.

"Forget about it," he said, staring at his phone.

"That's not the sort of thing that is easy to forget. Who's being haunted? Is it you?"

Ryan wished he had said nothing.

A plate of pasta was placed in front of him.

"Come on, then. You have my interest. I love this sort of stuff."

"I don't think you'd like this," he said.

"Try me." Eyes twinkling with curiosity, she downed some penne.

"It's either my phone or my flat," he said. "Or it could be Sharon's flat. I hear footsteps up there."

She dropped her fork on the table. "You mean to tell me the place I slept last night may be haunted? Are you kidding me?"

He was useless when it came to hiding secrets. He gave her a run-down of the messages on his phone.

"Let me see that." She took his phone and scrolled through screens and websites he had been on.

He wasn't concerned. He didn't do porn. He had nothing to hide. "Seems to happen at night mostly. Except this morning when it mentioned you." He instantly regretted revealing that detail. Idiot.

Eleanor's frown became a raised eyebrow.

"The phone said," he went on, "it was nice to meet you and to bring you back. Then it went back to normal." Hearing himself speak, he expected her to tell him to get out and, on account of being a nutcase, not come back.

But she didn't.

"I want to meet this ghost of yours," she said. "Get your dinner eaten and then let's get over to your place."

Ryan smiled with relief. A problem shared was more than halved as far as he was concerned. "Aren't you scared, though?"

"Of course, I am. I have just bedded my neighbour who happens to be haunted. That's a helluva first date. Let's make the second date even better."

Six

Ryan opened the door cautiously, letting his aura, if that was what he was doing, extend into the flat to see if anyone was there. Was there any presence?

Nothing. No hairs standing up on his arms. No trickle of fear down his neck. Sharon was still away and the whole property was empty. Coldish, but only because he hadn't been at home to turn on the heating.

He led the way into his flat and turned on the light. All was normal, the way he had left it that morning.

He could even smell a little of Eleanor's perfume, although with her standing beside him it may have been the real live smell.

"So," he said, "what are we going to do while we wait for the phone to do its thing?"

Eleanor led him to the bedroom and told him exactly what she wanted him to do. Ryan was more than willing. They fell asleep in each other's arms after an hour or so, satiated and happy. Phone on the bedside table.

He woke up to a claustrophobic white light glowing in the room. The hairs on his arms were raised. As he sat upright, he was breathing hard, sweating.

Eleanor was already awake and had his phone in her hands, staring at the screen.

"What does it say?"

"Someone wants to meet us."

"Can you respond? Type anything?"

"No," she said. "The screen is all fuzzy like you said. Seems to be a one-way conversation."

"I feel it. Can you? It's like there's another person in here right now. It goes away when the phone goes back to normal."

"The phone says they are not here with us."

After a brief pause, she looked at him and held the phone to his face so he could read it.

"I am upstairs. Would you like me to come down now? ☺"

Ryan was amazed. "The ghost has used a smiling

emoji."

Eleanor laughed. "Maybe the ghost has a sense of humour."

A resounding thump hit the ceiling upstairs.

Eleanor jumped, dropping the phone on the bed. Not much to laugh about after that bang.

Another thump. Then another, making its way across the ceiling towards the door that led to the stairs and the shared hallway.

Ryan grabbed his phone.

"See you shortly." No emojis this time.

Seven

"We should get out of here," Ryan said. "Who knows who or what is coming down the stairs. It's not Sharon, that's for sure."

The steps were coming down the stairs now. Loud hammers.

Ryan ran to his door, Eleanor by his side. "If we are quick, we can get out before it arrives."

He grabbed the handle but was too late. Knock, knock. Knuckles rapped the door as he turned the handle. Knock, knock.

He instinctively let go and jumped back, bowling Eleanor over, landing in a heap beside her.

They stared at the door as the handle slowly turned. The door swung inwards.

They scrambled back.

It was dark, the snowy phone illuminating the

room. It threw enough light at the doorway for them to see a shape.

A person.

Eleanor screamed. Ryan screamed. He wasn't the brave male ready to fight for his woman that he hoped he would be. He was too busy being terrified.

The shape stepped into the room slowly. No more thuds.

Eleanor stopped screaming. Ryan took his cue from her to do the same. His legs were useless, he had lost control of them, all he could do was watch. Rabbit in the headlights.

Eleanor scrambled to her feet.

The shape took another step forward and the ambient light of the phone caught the features.

It was a girl.

Teenager, wearing old workstyle clothes, things from years ago, normally only seen in black and white photos.

But not really a girl, either. You could see through bits of her, as though she was made from thin lace rather than skin and bone.

Her neck was constricted and black.

Her eyes were full of intelligence.

As the phone screen flickered, Ryan held it up.

"Hello, will you be my friends?" appeared on the screen.

As they looked at the girl, she stepped closer.

"What's your name?" Eleanor said. A bit loud for comfort.

The screen flickered again. "Florence."

Eleanor looked at Ryan. They were backed into the room. No running away.

"Hi, I'm Eleanor and this is Ryan."

The girl's head lolled almost off her shoulder as she surveyed them.

Ryan wanted to scream again but he had lost the ability to make a sound.

Thankfully, Eleanor had more composure. "Are you hurt?" Eleanor was all compassion. The teacher in her coming out at the sight of an injured child. Overcoming her own terror.

Ryan didn't know her that well but already he was getting the feeling she was a keeper. He was batting above his average, he thought. She was handling the situation so much better than him.

"Not anymore," the phone flickered.

"What happened?" Genuine concern.

Ryan still couldn't speak.

The girl's head stopped moving and recentred, looking at Eleanor. "They raped me. Then they strangled me and broke my neck."

Ryan nodded. Not sure what to think or say.

Eleanor was trained to work with young people. She was instinctively inclined to protect them. "Who did this to you, honey? Tell me."

His new girlfriend was having a conversation with a ghost.

Ryan was incredulous.

The mood was changing. He wondered how many

ghosts stopped to have a conversation with their victims before finishing them. Not many, if the movies were to be believed.

There was bubbling energy in the room. What he had taken for malevolence was now more like pent up anger. Or maybe it was sadness.

The phone flickered.

Eight

Florence did not say a word. Ryan was not sure the apparition could speak. It was disturbing to think that, even in death, the larynx may be crushed so bad. Or maybe it was a creepy ghost thing. The eyes watched all the time.

Florence spoke through the phone. Some of the spelling was a bit off but that was to be expected. She had only been fifteen when murdered and had left school a couple of years earlier.

Eleanor and Ryan sat together on the bed, the ghost of Florence standing two metres away while the screen flashed.

It was the early 1920s, not long after the Great War. She was from a poor working family living in this terraced house on Oxford Street. She lived in the upstairs flat.

She had brothers and sisters, who left school early to get jobs. She lied about her age when she was thirteen to get a cleaning job on the factory floor at the Timpson's shoe factory at North Park, near Bath

Road.

She worked there in the same job for two years. It was backbreaking, six or seven days a week for a pittance. She gave all her money to her mother and led a joyless life at home. Her father worked and was rarely home. Her mother raised six children in a two-bedroom flat. Food was expensive, clothes were repaired rather than replaced.

But Florence was happy. She had friends at Timpson's. Girls and boys her own age who she played with in the evenings or rare days off. They would go to the brook at Northfield Avenue and play games. She kissed a boy there, Alfie, who worked on the machines. It was enjoyable, she remembered.

When the three men waited for her to leave the factory on a cool winter's evening, they followed her and she was scared. It was dark, and when she took her usual cut through the poorly named Pleasure Park, they grabbed her.

She didn't know what was happening, didn't know to fight. It was nothing like kissing Alfie. They took turnabout raping her. She recognised their faces as they grunted on top of her, pain lancing between her legs, blood flowing. She knew them. Why were they doing this to her?

When finished, she lay there wondering what happened. She knew deep inside but was sore and shocked. One of them said, if she lived, then she could cause trouble. He strangled and broke her neck with powerful machinist hands.

They dumped her body in nearby wasteland and covered it with dirt. She watched from beside them as they did it. Surprised she could see it all. She knew she was dead. They left. Time passed and nobody found her. Nobody came to her rescue. No justice was ever delivered.

Eventually, she went home to Oxford Street. But it wasn't home anymore. Her family was gone. Moved. She had no feeling or sense of where they had gone. She never saw them again. She felt little emotion about it. They had raised and fed her. Clothed her. But there was little love to remember.

Ryan and Eleanor looked at each other. A life so different to theirs. They had their problems with work, bills, the cost of living, fitting into a world that never slept. But their problems were nothing compared to Florence.

Ryan hadn't been able to speak because of fear. Now it was sadness that constricted his chest. Injustice. Tears were running freely down his cheeks.

Eleanor was ashen white, face streaked wet with tears. "Why are you here with us? How can we help?"

"I have been alone for years," flashed the phone. "I didn't know how to speak to anyone until I found that machine in your hand. Anytime I ever showed myself people ran away. They even brought a priest to perform an exorcism. But it didn't work. I'm still here. I'm not a bad person. Now I am very bored. I don't want to be here anymore. Can you help me? Will you be my friends?"

Ryan and Eleanor looked at the shade of Florence, distended neck and ethereal presence. She wasn't as frightening as before. But she was out of place. Nature and instinct told them that. She had no place in the natural world. She was stuck here.

And it came to Ryan suddenly. He always had empathy and it was amped right now. He knew what to do.

He wiped tears from his face, took the phone and walked over to her. He was right beside her but there was no fear anymore. He wanted to help and the ghost sensed it. Florence's aura sensed it.

"Take the phone," he said holding it out. Her spirit hand took it. Ryan wasn't worried about the physics. Little made sense except she was a young innocent girl who had her life ripped away from her just as she was starting to really live. She had been lonely for a hundred years.

"I think you are here because you want to live a bit and maybe I can help you."

"What are you doing, Ryan?" Eleanor was beside him. He took her hand and gave it a squeeze. He turned to Florence. "Maybe if you live a little then you can move on to whatever comes next."

Florence knew he meant it. She nodded.

"That's a mobile phone. Most kids your age spend all day on them. You can learn so much about life and living through it. Why don't you use it. There are whole worlds inside it, you can travel the world. It will make you cry. You will wonder at the hate and be humbled by the love."

Florence looked at the phone.

"You can live a life through that phone. It's yours now. I just need to make sure it's charged. Do you want to give it a try? I'll be here if you need me."

Eleanor squeezed his hand.

Florence didn't smile but her spirit, her aura lifted. They both felt it.

Nine

Florence lived – if a ghost lives, that is – in the dining room of Ryan's flat for a full year. He put a table and chair in the corner and plugged the phone in for constant charge. He didn't know if she needed the chair, but she sat down, anyway.

When he got home from work, she would be sitting there. He would say hello and through the phone screen she said hello back.

While a word was never spoken, she used the phone to ask him about his day. She even helped him when he had problems. He would ask her advice. When Eleanor wanted to move in, Florence made it clear he would be stupid to say no. "She's the best thing to happen to you," said the phone screen. And Florence was right.

Eleanor had her own relationship with Florence and he would often hear her laughing when he was in the kitchen and she was with Florence in the dining room.

The three of them lived happily for that year. Never once would Ryan consider moving or selling up. Florence was like a little sister. Sometimes she quizzed him about the terrible inexplicable things happening in the news. They shared their frustrations and complete incomprehension of the constant injustice that so mirrored that of a hundred years ago. "History repeats itself, it is so sad," she told him. He could only agree.

He laughed with her when he found her watching an episode of *Family Guy*. Florence laughing was something to behold. Her head rolled around her shoulders at angles that were impossible for anyone living, but she assured them it was not painful. For a while they watched episodes together on an iPad in the evenings.

It felt like family time.

Florence was amazed at modern food, air travel and space flights. She was childlike in her wonder.

One day, they watched an episode of *South Park* together and laughed a lot. Florence got it.

Then, like a flick of a switch, the atmosphere changed. Florence approached them both and handed the phone to Ryan.

"Thank you," flickered on the screen.

Ryan cried. Whimpering, Eleanor grabbed his hand. Neither had children but they knew what was coming.

"I have had a wonderful time living with you. But now it is time for me to move on. You have made that possible. Know that I love you both and will take your love with me. Thank you."

The flickering screen returned to normal.

Florence was gone.

Ryan felt alone. Desolate.

Then Eleanor was hugging him tight, tears soaking his chest.

Ryan was not alone.

About the Authors

Pat Aitcheson has been an active member of Northants Writers' Ink for ten years and writing stories even longer. She previously achieved first prize in the H E Bates Short Story Competition and a long list place in the Bath Novel Award.

Her writing credits include contributions to four of the group's previous anthologies as well as anthologies by the Wee Free Writers and The Creative Cafe, and a local monthly magazine *Barton Today*.

Having retired from a career in healthcare, she seeks future writing inspiration in her Northamptonshire garden, art and travel.

Deborah Bromley is a writer of paranormal fiction who uses experiences gained in her hypnotherapy practice, including past life and life-between-lives regression, to inspire her writing.

She discovered the pleasure of writing short stories after joining Northants Writers' Ink and is currently the group's Secretary.

Two collections of her short stories have been

published: *Challenges from the Writers' Group* and *The Importance of Vests*.

Deborah has also written and recorded three guided meditation titles for Hemi-Sync® (hemi-sync.com). *Creating a Positive Future*, *Calm and Peaceful* and *Slimmer and Healthier* are available for download or in CD format from the Hemi-Sync® website. *Slimmer and Healthier,* a twelve-track album series, is accompanied by a companion book of the same title.

Gemma Croucher was born and bred in the depths of South-East London. She, along with her husband and two children, moved to a quiet village in Northamptonshire in 2011.

From a young child, she has had an unwavering love for books and reading which lead to a fifteen-year career as a secondary school English teacher. She has since re-trained and is in the process of setting up her own business.

Struck by the idea for a novel one day, she turned her hand to writing, joining Northants Writers' Ink in 2023. The group has been invaluable to her in terms of moral support, skill development and constructive critiquing.

Gemma's short story included in this anthology is her first published work. She hopes to self-publish her first novel in the not-too-distant future.

Ashley Holthofer writes:

For this anthology, I contributed a short story,

Moving On. If you took the time to read it, I am grateful. If you enjoyed it, then know that it makes me very happy that others are able to derive joy from my work.

Moving On is my first publication. It is also the first piece I have seriously presented to others. I have no writing accolades to speak of. That being said, I write prolifically in my spare time and have written many short stories.

Over the past three years, I have been working on a novel titled *Invader*, a story of love and tragedy in wartime Poland.

After paying a ludicrous amount of money for a below-average master's in creative writing, **Kris Longden** has spent the last few years attempting to wrestle his début novel into shape. In the meantime, he's found other, more successful, outlets for his writing. These include contributing stories to Northants Writers' Ink and writing less exciting words in his day job.

Jason McClean writes:

I first wrote stories when I was at school. That was over 40 years ago. I did it for pleasure, but it also helped me work out truths about life. As I grew up, writing and reading helped me form early opinions and work out what was important.

My first story was read out at a writers' group in the Linenhall Library in Belfast. It majored on lost love and the suicide of the soul. That theme remains relevant today.

I made it as a published author when I co-wrote the autobiography of triple British Superbike Champion John Reynolds. A great life story and 10,000 copies were printed. My commercial writing peak.

I joined Northants Writers' Ink and found a group of like-minded writers who supported and encouraged me. It's been great fun since. I have written more than fifty stories and contributed to previous anthologies. My personal writing peak.

I am still writing and reading to form opinions and work out what is important. Now closer to retirement than school, I've found the older I get, the more I need writing to help me work out real truths about life.

Jethro Punter has been a member of Northampton Writers' Ink for the last five years, joining during the Covid-19 lockdown. Writing assignments for the group provided a welcome way to escape the four walls of his home.

Since that time, he has written a wide range of stories: long, short and in-between, covering everything from a modern-day fairy tale of a lonely peacock to imagining a world where every conspiracy theory has come true. All the while, he has taken the opportunity to learn and develop as a writer with the help and advice of the group.

Jethro has published a fantasy middle grade series *The Daydreamer Chronicles*, a winner in the Wishing Shelf Awards for Children's Fiction. He has also published an urban fantasy noir series *The Judas Investigations* for older readers under the pen name Edward Rose.

One series features an impossibly giant staircase in the centre of the world, the other a huge elevator. There is probably something psychological going on behind it all, but he's not sure what.

Jo Purdon grew up near Heathrow Airport and left school at sixteen with no further education. She moved to Wellingborough in her late teens but didn't start writing until she was fifty.

Joining a writers' group was a steep learning curve but, supported and challenged by fellow members of Northants Writers' Ink, her writing improved and her confidence grew.

She contributed three short stories to the previous anthology, *Soft Shadows, Faint Footprints.*

In June 2024, she published her first novel under the pseudonym Jaime Southwark. *Beneath the Neon Lights* is a dark and gritty coming-of-age story about a teenage rent boy, inspired by a newspaper article Jo read in the 1980s. The book is available from Amazon.

She is currently working on the sequel and plans to publish a book of short stories in the near future.

Michael J Richards is the founder Chair of Northants Writers' Ink and Chair of Northampton Writers Group. He is also a member of The Alliance of Independent Authors.

He has published eight books: *Afterwards Our Buildings Shape Us*, a comic horror novel; *Bodies for Sale!*, a collection of 20 horror, crime and sci-fi stories; *Frank Peters: his life, times and crimes*, a true crime biography of an East End gangster; *Speaking Man to Man*, a collection of 20 stories about men; *All This and Everything Else Too*, a collection of 20 stories; *Meanwhile, in the Shadows*, a collection of 20 horror and crime stories; *Learnin' the Family Business*, a family saga set in New York; *The Randomness of Murder*, a collection of stories, each featuring at least one murder.

He has edited, among others, seven anthologies. For Northants Writers' Ink: *Tales of the Scorpion*; *While Glancing out of a Window*; *Talking Without Being Interrupted*; *And Ghosts Are Real Too*; *Soft Shadows, Faint Footprints*; *In This County...* For Northampton Literature Group: *If You Speak of Love*.

Michael J Richards is available for speaking engagements, workshops, book groups and similar. He can be contacted at mjrichardsauthor@gmail.com

Allan Shipham is a founder member of Northants Writer's Ink and lives in Wellingborough.

Writing was something Allan always found a challenge but, with perseverance and support from the group, he's developed and enjoys it a great deal. He hopes his contributions to our anthologies keep you entertained but also inspire you.

Allan's love of science fiction and an archive photo of workmen exhuming graves to widen a street in the town inspired *Introducing Master Ajax Ambrose*. He hopes it spikes your interest and leads you to explore more about the history of where you live.

Tracy Smith writes:

I am a self-employed bookkeeper who likes to write stories in her spare time. Now that my children are grown up with families of their own, I have more time available for writing. I always imagined as a child that I would become an author one day and so I decided to find out if it was possible.

I joined Northants Writers' Ink a few years ago and the support, inspiration and confidence I've gained as a result have been invaluable. This is the second time I've contributed to a Northants Writers' Ink anthology.

I am currently working on my own book, a collection of short stories that I hope will be ready for publication by Spring 2026.

Christopher J Wright has been a member of Northants Writers' Ink for nine years and is its Treasurer. As both a reader and a writer, he is drawn to science fiction, although NWI has helped broaden his horizons.

His stories have appeared in three of the group's previous anthologies: *Soft Shadows, Faint Footprints; And Ghosts are Real Too; Talking Without Being Interrupted.*

He has published *The Enodia Enigma*, a science fiction mystery following an anthropologist and a navy lieutenant as they separately piece together the discovery of a threat to humanity. It is available from Amazon.

And Ghost Are Real Too
an anthology
by Northants Writers' Ink

Evil lurks in 10thC Wendelingburgh • Six men encounter horror in the Tithe Barn, Wendelingburgh • The soul of a Gunpowder Plot leader visits a little girl in Isham • A young man is transported back to the Battle of Naseby • The Witchfinder General interrogates the husband of a Northampton witch • 19thC Kirby Hall has an unwelcome visitor and a ghostly haunting • A cackling witch terrorises people in Wellingborough • A teenage girl communicates with spirits from the beyond.

All this and more in *And Ghosts Are Real Too*, an anthology of thirteen stories with a difference. Every story is a tale of ghosts, horror or crime, all set in the English county of Northamptonshire.

They are scary, shocking and authentic.

This is the fourth anthology by Northants Writers' Ink, a group based in Wellingborough, England.

What they said…

Have been introduced to this group of writers through a friend, and I have found some great reads. The book comprises a selection of different authors with great writing styles. I thoroughly enjoyed all the stories within the book but found Chris Wright's "Shelter from the Storm" and Pat Aitcheson's "Will Ye Choose to Live?" particularly gripping. Well worth a read!

I got this book as a recommendation/present from a friend and it really deserved its place on my bookshelf. I especially like the stories by one of the younger writers, James William Dart, and his second story in the book "The Betrayal" really surprised me and terrified me in unexpected ways. Definitely worth purchasing to support local talent around Northamptonshire, or if you just like short stories with a little bit of horror.

An absorbing and stimulating anthology of stories. A varied and unique selection. Some of these tales, set in Northamptonshire, particularly compelled me to read on. They are fine examples of the craft of storytelling: "Will" by Michael J Richards; "The Betrayal" by James Dart and "Shelter from the Storm" by Chris Wright are my favourites. All the pieces of work here captured my imagination and entertained me. Well presented and organised, this is a book I will return to and reread. Brilliant.

A slim volume of stories, fictional, but based on the area around Wellingborough. Lots of different styles which was enjoyable. My favourites, Nick Wogden's Wellingborough Witch stories, which were very well written and hit the spot, for me.

I liked this short collection of ghost horror and crime stories set in Northamptonshire for the mix of writing styles on show. I also liked the local references which will be of interest to any reader who lives in or near Northants.

Available from Amazon either directly or via www.northantswritersink.co.uk.

If you order from Northants Writers' Ink via northantswritersink@outlook.com, your copies will be signed.

Soft Shadows, Faint Footprints
an anthology
by Northants Writers' Ink

Soft Shadows, Faint Footprints is an affectionate, wonderfully varied anthology of short stories set in Northamptonshire.

It explores the county's rich history, its present day, looks forward to its future and re-introduces some long-lost ghosts.

Follow Edward I as he builds Eleanor Crosses in memory of his beloved queen. Sit before Charles I in Holdenby House as he contemplates his execution. Find out what happened when Northampton was bombed in World War Two.

Experience the world of professional wrestling. Meet a community of ghosts. See what Northamptonshire will look like when robots take over.

All this and much, much more in *Soft Shadows, Faints Footprints*. This is an anthology by Northants Writers' Ink, a writers group based in Wellingborough, Northamptonshire.

What they said…

Short stories provide a perfect reading experience, particularly when there is so much variety. I thoroughly enjoyed the historical tales and I thought the story about Charles I was really well written. I also enjoyed the story about Northampton's underworld, "Trapped in a Memory" by Jethro Punter.

If you like short stories this is a lovely read. My favourite is "FearTube" by Tracy Smith.

A really good read, full of a variety of stories and writing styles. Really enjoyed the Northamptonshire theme from local writers.

This lively anthology offers a variety of short stories from a Northamptonshire-based writers group, each story telling its own tale, completely separate from the others but all with the common thread of being set in or around Northampton, and presented in 4 sections covering the past, present and future – and a further 2 stories under the heading "In the Beyond".

Drawn into the depths of history, we see King Edward, heartbroken at losing his beloved Eleanor; King Charles I held prisoner in Holdenby House; a WW2 RAF plane crashes in Northampton… and much more.

The present-day section treats us to a mixed bag of topics including bullying, a fated wedding, human trafficking, an old clock that finds its way home, and a witty and crushingly satirical peek into the lives of the "country set". Into the future, we find body dumping, robots in control and an elderly chap getting the better of the taxman.

The book closes with 2 tales of – well, something rather other-worldly!

All in all, a great little compilation, every story interesting and entertaining in its own right, whether history, romance, humour, mystery, drama, or that intriguing "other-worldly" bit!

Highly recommended, definitely well worth a read.

Soft Shadows, Faint Footprints is an entertaining testament to the writing talent waiting to be discovered by those willing to take a step away from the well-trodden path. It's a diverse mix of short stories, all set in Northamptonshire's past, present and possible futures.

Without fail, the stories grabbed and held the attention. But two that stood out for me were "No Hold Barred" by James Dart, revealing a dark side to the world of professional wrestling, and "Circles" by Jo Purdon, a touching reminiscence by an aged woman as she leaves her home for the final time.

I thoroughly enjoyed reading this anthology, some of the stories are laugh out loud funny, some deeply poignant, some an intriguing insight into subjects I had no previous knowledge of. All the stories are just the right length and are written about subjects the authors obviously care a lot about. I don't live in Northamptonshire but I thoroughly enjoyed the book, it's a great read – I highly recommend it!

These stories really are each the perfect length. I particularly enjoyed the contribution by Deborah Bromley which is set in a believable arm's length future. Interesting, intriguing but also unsettling to read. Great fun. You are left wanting for more.

These short stories are packed with real detail about towns and places in Northants. Whether in the past, present or future, these stories delight. Thought provoking and cleverly written, whether you are walking down memory lane, looking for love or to the future, each story is bite size to reading one sitting and well worth the time. Try out the other anthologies by this group as well, excellent reading.

This anthology is packed with well-written, diverse and thoroughly entertaining stories. My favourites include: "The prisoner king" by Chris Wright; "What we do when we talk about our lives" by Michael J Richards and "No holds barred" by James Dart. Very accessible and well presented. I highly recommend this book.

Soft Shadows, Faint Footprints is an anthology of short

stories written within set parameters. The tales are written with skill and inventiveness. They all capture the reader's attention. Jo Purdon, a talented new writer, presents three stories. Her characters come to life off the page. One story struck a personal and emotional chord with me: I instantly recalled memories of unexpected kindness and love, in a warring world of harshness and frugality. I highly recommend this book.

Loved this book. Really like the four sections – past, present, future and beyond. Particularly liked the take on the royal execution and the ghosts of the long canal tunnels. I'd like to read more from Tracy Smith.

Great collection of short stories for easy reading! The variety in each writers style keeps you interested and intrigued to read the next.

I loved these short stories. I particularly liked the fact that it was local stories and the way it was divided into Past, Present, Future, and Beyond. I liked "Daisy" and the fact that it was based on the memories of the author's mother. I also liked the way "A red rose for love" about the Eleanor Crosses was written in resting sequence, not chronologically. All the stories were good – it's almost impossible to pick out favourites.

This is a wonderful and varied collection of short

stories, based in the past, present and future. What will make it particularly interesting to anyone living in Northamptonshire or nearby, is that all of the stories are set in that part of the UK. Hence we have stories referencing Irthlingborough, Wellingborough, Thrapston, Castle Ashby, Biddenham and Stoke Bruerne, for example. This book is a must for any local, and of interest to any lover of short fiction!

Available from Amazon either directly or via www.northantswritersink.co.uk.

If you order from Northants Writers' Ink via northantswritersink@outlook.com, your copies will be signed.

Printed in Dunstable, United Kingdom